SWISH

1996

By

William Thomas London

FREE PREVIEW

When he got on campus, he noticed a crowd gathering at the Quad in the middle of the campus. There was a lot of joking and laughter going on. As he approached, he saw amongst the crowd laughing harder than anyone was Freeze.

"What's so funny?" He inquired of his friend, Freeze, as he approached him.

Freeze answered him and said to him, "Dude." He spurted out between his laughter.

He greeted JJ with a high five.

"You late, dude." He said to JJ, trying to control his laughter.

"What?" JJ asked him.

"You missed out on the fun, look," Freeze said to him, pointing towards the flagpole in the right corner of the Quad.

There hanging from the flagpole, was a human body. It was the pale, weird-looking kid.

"Momma!" The weird kid yelled out.

"Momma!" The crowd yelled out mocking him.

"Ain't that the funniest thing you've ever seen?" Freeze asked JJ.

"The funniest thing," JJ repeated to Freeze halfheartedly because he was not really feeling this joke.

"Momma!" The boy yelled out again.

His underwear showed as the hook from the flagpole rope bungled his blue underwear into a wedgie. His pants were down to his ankles now, and his shirt was covering his pale face.

"Momma!" The weird-looking boy yelled out again.

This time the rope had rotated the boy so that he was facing the crowd. His shirt had fallen to the ground. You could see the tears streaming down from his face.

Somehow JJ did not see the humor in this prank anymore.

"Ok, Freeze, that's enough," JJ said to Freeze.

"Let him down."

KEYNOTE

Swish is an inner-city adventure book that takes place in the 1990s. The story takes a serious look at adolescent bullying in High School.

To the young men I have mentored over the years:

Ecclesiastes 11:9 ESV

Rejoice, O young man, in your youth, and let your heart cheer you in the days of your youth. Walk in the ways of your heart and the sight of your eyes. But know that for all these things, God will bring you into judgment.

Mae Ellen Davis Wright

My parents:

William Leo and Amanda Ellen (Thompkins) Wright

Ephesians 6:1 NIV

Children obey your parents in the Lord, for this is right.

Rev William Leo "Willie" Wright, Sr.

Amanda Ellen Thompkins Wright

My Grandparents

[Paternal] Jimmy and Moase "Moose" Coleman Wright"

I will now praise the godly, our ancestors, in their downtime,

Sirach 44:1 USCCB

Jimmy Wright, Sr.

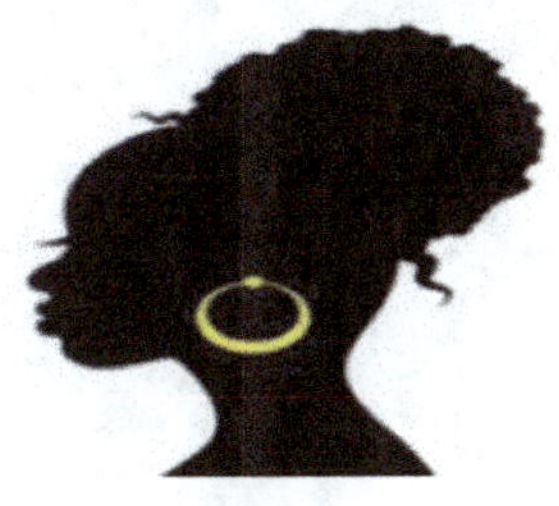

Moase (Moose) Coleman Wright

Jessie Terrell Lucas Thompkins and Claude Thompkins

My siblings who have gone on to glory:

Marian Yvonne Wright

Katherine (Wright) Johnson

Lewis Rochelle Wright

Deborah (Wright) Gaston

Thomas (Lil Pookie) Curtis Wright

Dorothy (Dot) Jean (Wright) Dodds

Carrie E. Wright

 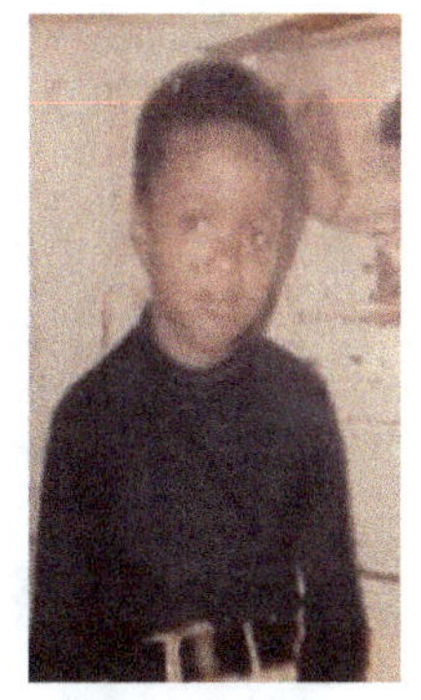

Marian Yvonne Wright   Lewis Rochelle Wright Thomas   (Lil Pookie) Curtis Wright

Katherine Wright Johnson   Deborah Wright Gaston   Dorothy Jean "Dot" Wright Dodds

Carrie Ellen Wright

My siblings who are still on this journey with me:

William L. Wright, Jr.

Willette A.

(Wright) Jones

Carl B. Wright Sr.   Ruth M. (Wright) Broach

Dr. Dale H. Conaway

Hebrews 13:1-2 NIV

Keep on loving one another as brothers and sisters. Do not forget to show hospitality to strangers, for by so doing, some people have shown hospitality to angels without knowing it.

My Church Family

Allen Temple Missionary Baptist Church

8501 International Blvd. Oakland, Ca. 94621

Matthew 18:20-22

New King James Version

[20] For where two or three are gathered (A)together in My name, I am there in the midst of them.

Shout out to:

My Former Coworkers:

Alameda County Probation Department (Camp Sweeney)

Oakland Unified School District (Stonehurst & Howard Elementary Schools) Oakland Parks and Recreation.

Staff and Patients at:

Fresenius Kidney Care Stockton, California, where this book was written.

To the Staff of:

Weston Ranch Library Stockton California where some of this book was written.

Matthew 9:37

New International Version

[37] Then he said to his disciples, "The harvest is plentiful, but the laborers are few."

SPECIAL THANKS

My niece, Jonnette Marvetta "Nettie" Jones, for lending her creative talents in creating pictures for this book.

My sister, Willette Wright Jones, for assisting, editing, arranging, and helping me complete this project.

Lonnie, you asked for my opinion so here is my two cents worth of critique.

Our parents would be very proud of you and your accomplishments. Now, you know if Mama were here, I'd have to tell on you for using "cuss words" and she would have disciplined you with a sound spanking using the switch you had to go and pick off the tree in the backyard yourself.

Overall, I feel your story captures what many people like Benjamin "Swish" Swisher experience in life. Through adversity, they are able to thrive every day even though they are being bullied and ridiculed just for being who they are. The "Swish" character was innocent and humble as well as brave enough to persevere through the challenges presented to him and was able to teach many life lessons to those who took the time to get to know him. He was also multi-talented and had a great sense of humor.

Actually, the character reminds me of you.

Willette Amanda Wright Jones

My brother-in-law, John R. Jones, Sr. for assistance with picture arrangements and editing.

Uzbekistan

Table of Contents

SWISH
1995

CHAPTER 1 NEW ON THE BLOCK

Here he was at the podium of his graduation day.

June 12th, 1996. One day before his 18th birthday. Reflecting upon what had really happened that year. Preparing to give the valedictorian speech for his class.

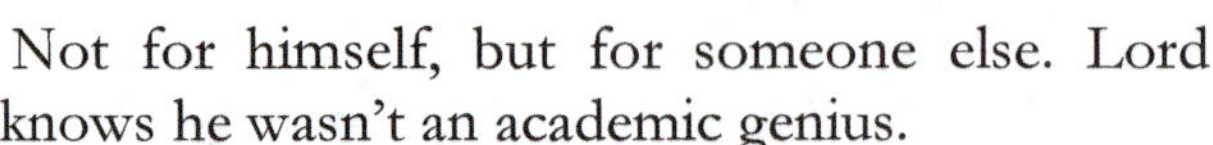

Not for himself, but for someone else. Lord knows he wasn't an academic genius.

He was giving it to someone more deserving than himself.

A special person that had changed the way he looked at life.

He was giving the speech in his stead. Surely an honor.

As he stood there waiting to speak, he reflected upon how they had come to this moment. It seemed so long ago.

The year was September 1995. The beginning of his Senior year at Amanda Ellen Thompkins Senior High. The year started off like every other year.

The vice principal was Ulysses Jackson. Mr. J for short.

He was a big burly Black guy with a fluffy natural going bald in the middle. The only thing bushier than that Afro with the hole in the middle was that thick mustache and beard on his scraggly unshaven face.

Everyone at the school knew he was the real principal.

Next, there was the principal, Mr. Alex Johnson. A timid, scrawny, White guy whose, petite stature matched his soft-spoken voice.

He was short and pale. He had a clean-shaven face, with thin brown hair, that was graying on the edges.

His skin was white as snow. Unlike Mr. Jackson, who was on a bullhorn in the hallways all about campus, constantly barking out marching orders. Mr. Johnson kept himself pretty much hidden in his office.

The school year started off with the same boring routine.

Monday was freshman orientation day, Tuesday was school assembly, Wednesday and Thursday were class sign-up days, and Friday was teacher prep day.

JJ, being a jock, with his classes already chosen for him, just came to school to hang out. He had a letter in three sports: baseball, football, and basketball.

He just came to school to hang out with the homies, flirt with the honeys, and pick on the nerds, the dweebs.

He basically hung out frolicking with the basketball team. They have had a special connection since elementary school.

There was Morris Green, Big Mo, the 6'8" center. He was Lanky as a giraffe, but clumsy as an ox.

He was the only one at the school who had an Afro bigger than Mr. Jackson's, (minus the hole in the middle.)

There was Dwight "Da White Boi", Rogers. The only White guy on the basketball team. (Though according to him, he was an octogenarian.)

"Why do you think I got curly hair?" He would proclaim to everyone.

There was Javier Guerrero. (AKA the Latin Lover). He was their namesake. (Often the group of them were known as Guerrero's Posse.)

Javier was a thin, dark-skinned, Latino guy, who was a ladies' man.

Finally, there was Kevin Foster (also known as "Freeze") the shooting guard.

He along with Jonathan Jenkins (known as JJ), the point guard, made up the backcourt of the team.

Their nickname was the run-and-gun twins. People often said they couldn't tell them apart – two 5'9" brothers, 150 lbs., medium Afros, same swag, same jive talk.

They were inseparable. Even during the summer months, they hung out with each other.

The whole team together called themselves the AT posse.

"We ride together, we die together, I am my brother's keeper," was their motto.

"Where the breezies' at, J Dog?" Freeze yelled over to JJ, as he approached him from across the Quad.

"In the cafeteria," JJ yelled back to him, as he gave Freeze a dap, a fist pound, and a manly hug.

"Well, that's where I be at. You coming, dude" Freeze asked JJ.

"Be there in a minute. I got to go over here to the office and see my counselor, Mr. T." (The name they had for Mr. Thomas, the resource counselor.) JJ told Freeze.

"Ok, bro'. Holla' at you later." Freeze said to JJ.

The two went their separate ways. Freeze went to the cafeteria while JJ went to the office.

As JJ entered the office, he was asked to have a seat by one of the office secretaries, Miss Summers, an elderly frail White lady who wore her metal-rimmed glasses on her nose.

"Wait there." She said to him, pointing to one of the seats in the corner of the room.

While he waited, he couldn't help but notice Principal Johnson in a heated argument in his office with a parent. He strained to get the 411 on what was happening.

"My son is just as smart as the rest of these kids." The lady insisted to Mr. Johnson.

The voice came from a thin Black lady, heavily clad in clothing, considering the temperature that day was more than seventy-five degrees.

She had a high-pitched, almost squeaky voice and a stare that could stop an elephant in its tracks.

"Well, Miss Swisher. Your son comes to us from a special education program. Now, if he can't pass the remedial test, we have to put him in the class for special needs pupils." Mr. Johnson informed her.

"Nonsense." She said to him, pointing to a piece of paper on the table with her long sharp index finger.

She then said to him, "Look at his test scores."

The young man they talked about stood about four feet nine. Small in stature. Couldn't have been more than 110 lbs. wet.

And pale. I mean paler than pale. He had a short flaming red Afro with two bald patches on the sides.

He was whiter than "Da White Boi." Albino. Freckle faced.

JJ stood close to Mr. Johnson's office door trying to eavesdrop on what was going on.

"Jenkins." JJ jumped at the sound of his name being called.

Although Mr. Thomas, the resource counselor, had whispered his name, the intensity of his trying to hear what was going on in the principal's office caught JJ off guard. The silence was broken like a lightning bolt hitting a tree in a thunderstorm.

He jumped to attention at the sound of his name being called.

JJ stood before a round, pudgy White man who appeared to be wider than he was tall. He wore a green suit and a black tam. He looked more like an overweight leprechaun than a counselor.

"Come on in my office." Mr. Thomas told him to do as he motioned JJ to him by waving his right hand.

Slowly, JJ moved towards Mr. Thomas's office. As he entered the office, Mr. Thomas motioned for JJ to have a seat in a chair in front of his desk.

Not once did he make eye contact with JJ. He kept reading a folder he held in front of his face and kept making sounds as if he were having a conversation with himself.

Uh-hum. Uh-hum." He kept saying to himself.

In between, his uh hums there were some sporadic, "D's."

Finally, he looked at JJ and said to him in his coarse voice, "Son, you do plan to go to college, don't you?"

Now the students learned, that no matter what your intentions were, the answer to this question was, "Yes".

Otherwise, you would be subjected to an hour-long speech on how you were wasting your potential.

"Yes, sir," JJ answered him.

"Well, according to your transcripts, you need a math class and a science class." Mr. Thomas informed JJ.

"So, I am going to cut two of your electives and add these classes to your transcript." He told JJ.

Not wanting to show his disappointment, JJ stood up and put a big grin on his face. He shook Mr. Thomas's hand and he eagerly said to him, "Thank you, sir. Will that be it, sir?"

"Yes, son. That will be it. Carry on." Mr. Thomas told JJ.

"That boy got a good head on his shoulders." JJ heard Mr. Thomas reply as JJ scampered out of his office.

JJ wanted to quickly get back outside of Mr. Johnson's office, where the little thin, Black lady and Mr. Johnson were discussing the weird kid's fate.

"Amazing." JJ heard Mr. Johnson say as JJ approached Mr. Johnson's office.

"Fascinating." He heard Mr. Jackson say, as he held a piece of paper in front of his face.

By now, an array of faculty members were in the office spurting out a bunch of, "oohs" and "aahs".

"What do you think." Mr. Johnson inquired of Mr. Jackson.

"Well, the boy got every answer right on the proficiency exam. That's gotta be a first." Mr. Jackson replied as he handed the paper back to Mr. Johnson.

Mr. Johnson looked at the lady and he said to her, "Well, ma'am. I guess you have proved your point. Regular classes for your son."

"Well, bout time you said something that made sense." The lady said to him, as she turned to exit the office.

"Come on, Benji." She told the strange-looking boy.

The strange-looking boy followed her out of the office with a stiff gait, still twiddling his fingers and making faces.

JJ exited the office and went towards the Quad, where he tried to find Freeze.

He spotted Freeze under the oak tree in the middle of the campus.

"Hey, Freeze," JJ yelled to him as he got Freeze's attention.

"Hey, convict," Freeze replied to him.

"You survived the Warden's office, I see. What does Mr. Thomas want?" Freeze inquired of JJ.

"Just to change some of my classes around," JJ answered him.

"Oh, one of those we want you to reach your full potential speeches, huh?" Freeze said to JJ.

"Yeah, pretty much," JJ said to Freeze as he chuckled.

"Hey, you should have seen the dweeb who was in the office, new kid," JJ said to Freeze.

"What new kid?" Freeze asked JJ.

Just as he had spoken, the new kid exited the office with his mother.

The sun glistened off of his pale and his bright red hair looked like it was afire.

"That kid over there," JJ said to Freeze, as he pointed out the new kid.

Freeze turned in the direction JJ was pointing in and he said to JJ, "What the hell?"

For a moment, Freeze stood there mesmerizing at the funny-looking boy. He then got a mischievous grin on his face.

"You know what I'm thinking?" Freeze said to JJ.

"No, what are you thinking?" JJ replied to Freeze.

Freeze looked at the flagpole nodding his head.

First, JJ looked at the flagpole confused, trying to figure out what Freeze was thinking about.

He then remembered it was a school tradition for the seniors to grab nerds and hang them on the flagpole on the first day of school.

"Oh, no. I don't want any parts of that. Remember last year? Some seniors almost got expelled." He reminded Freeze.

"C'mon, now. It will be fun. Besides the seniors last year were a bunch of dummies. We gonna get away wit' it, fo' sho'." Freeze replied to JJ.

"Look, buddy. You on your own on this one." JJ told Freeze.

"Suit yourself. When the first day of school starts, I am gonna have some fun." Freeze told JJ.

"Suit yourself, homie. I am going to sit this one out. I can't afford to be expelled." JJ told Freeze.

The two high-fived each other and went their separate ways.

CHAPTER 2 THE CHALLENGE

The next day was Saturday. JJ slept in late. It was about noon when his mother woke him up.

"Pookie." His mother called him by the pet name she had for him.

"Get up boy." The little, short, plump, brown-skinned lady said to him, as she shook him out of his sleep.

"Get up boy. You got company." She said again in her deep contralto voice.

JJ sat up on the bed and rubbed his eyes. He then laid back down and pulled the covers back over himself.

"I said get up, didn't I." She repeated herself to him.

This time in a sharper voice.

"You got company." She said to him again.

"Ma, what I tell you about calling me that in front of my friends." He told her referring to the pet name she had given him.

"Boy, I was in labor with you for eight hours. I will call you anything I want." She said to him, as he mouthed the words out of her mouth to mock her.

"Get up you knock." He heard a familiar voice yell out to him.

He recognized the person as his friend, Freeze.

Freeze came rushing through the door and he sat next to him on the bed.

"Get up, boy. We got to get our hustle on." Freeze told JJ.

"Get up and get your clothes on." He said, as he pulled the covers back off of JJ and swatted his friend on the rear end.

JJ was lying on his side, on his bed, in a fetal position. He was clad in his boxers and socks only.

"Ok, ok, I'm up," JJ said sitting up on the bed.

"Damn, can't a brotha' get some sleep around here?" JJ complained to Freeze.

"Nah, bruh'. Not as long as it's sick money out there to be landed. We already missed out on a couple of hunned', playa'." Freeze told him.

"Now get up, P-o-o-k-i-e," Freeze said to him, as he dragged out the pronunciation of JJ's pet name his mother had for him. He did it purposely so as to irritate his friend.

"Alright, I'm up," JJ told him, as he got up and sat up on the side of his bed.

"And stop calling me that." JJ insisted on Freeze.

"Stop calling you what?" Freeze asked JJ.

JJ looked at Freeze with a stern, silent stare.

"Oh, you mean Pookie?" Freeze told him with a big grin on his face.

JJ remained silent. He just nodded his head with a frown on his face.

"Pookie, Pookie," Freeze said teasing JJ.

JJ began swinging at Freeze.

"You missed. Missed again. Close that time." Freeze said, taunting JJ as he dodged each blow JJ threw at him.

Finally, Freeze tackled JJ on the bed and held him down.

"Hey, c'mon, bruh'. Save some of that energy for the B-Ball game." Freeze told JJ.

"Get off me, bruh'!" JJ yelled at Freeze, as he shrugged Freeze off of him.

JJ got up and went to the bathroom, where he brushed his teeth, and did a five-minute wash up at the sink.

He then threw on some shorts, a tee shirt, some socks, and some tennis shoes. He was all ready to go in 15 minutes.

They both set out for the neighborhood park.

"So, what's the plan, man?" Freeze asked JJ.

"I don't know. What's the plan? You the perky one with all the energy." JJ replied to Freeze.

"OK, the way I see it. We bet everything we got when we played Ray Ray and Stimpy. They never beat us.

Same thing with Lil Z and Malcolm. They never beat us, either.

Last, when we play Big Baby and Slim, we bet half. We haven't beaten them, yet." Freeze strategized with JJ.

The two agreed with this plan. They soon arrived at the basketball courts.

When they arrived at the park, their competition had already arrived. They were there waiting for them.

As planned they played Ray Ray and Stimpy first. As expected they beat them.

They also won the next game against Lil Z and Malcolm.

So far, they have stuck with their game plan and they have doubled their money. About time they finished the first two games, they had won two hundred dollars.

Now it was time for the game against Big Baby and Slim. They only bet half of what they had won.

Big Baby and Slim were totally opposites of each other.

Slim was a light-skinned brother, with wavy brown hair. He stood about 5'9" and had a slender build. He was the smack talker of the two.

Big Baby, on the other hand, was low-keyed. He stood about 6'5", and was a dark-skinned brother, with a close-cut hairdo and a muscular build like a Black Adonis. He was the quiet one of the two.

"We betting a hunned." Freeze said to Slim, as he threw in a wad of balled-up $20s into the pot.

"A hunned it is," Slim answered Freeze back, as he confirmed the bet and he counted out and he straightened out five $20 bills and added them to the pot.

True to form, Slim began his smack talk before the game got started. He knew Freeze's weakness was his pride.

"Oh, I understand. Y'all' scared. Why don't y'all bet the whole two hunned?" Slim challenged them to do.

Freeze and JJ remained silent.

"Y'all know. Y'all gonna' lose, huh? I understand. Playing it safe." Slim said to them, as he continued to agitate Freeze.

"Naw, we not gonna' lose," Freeze told him, as Slim finally got under his skin.

"Here, the whole two hunned ducats. Y'all going down." Freeze proclaimed to Slim, as he threw the other hundred onto the pile.

"What you doing, man?" JJ whispered to Freeze as Freeze walked back towards him.

"No worries, dude. I got this." Freeze told JJ.

Freeze then specified the rules of the game.

"We going to twenty-four by twos. Got to win by fo'." Freeze told Slim.

"Winners take out," Freeze added.

"That's fine with me," Slim told Freeze.

They looked at JJ and Big Baby.

JJ remained silent. He just nodded his head in agreement.

Big Baby showed everyone a thumbs up.

"Here, y'all take the ball out first. Seeing this the last time y'all gonna' touch the ball." Slim bragged to them, as he was laughing.

"We will be shirts. Y'all be skins." Slim added.

JJ and Freeze took their shirts off and threw them to the side of the court.

JJ started off the game by passing the ball into Freeze.

For the next thirty minutes, they played a fierce game in which the lead changed hands a couple of times.

With the score Shirts, twenty-two, Skins, twenty, Freeze had the ball.

He was dribbling the ball in the far-right corner of the court, with Slim guarding him. Once again, Slim played to Freeze's ego.

"Shoot the ball. You scared?" Slim asked him, as he dared Freeze to shoot the ball.

The two had been trash-talking the whole game.

"The only thing I'm scared of is yo' mama," Freeze told Slim, as he trash-talked back to him.

Freeze stopped dribbling the ball and stood in the far-right-hand corner of the court.

"Shoot the ball," Slim yelled to Freeze, challenging him to take a shot.

"You scared, huh?" Slim added.

"No, pass the ball. That's not your shot." JJ reminded Freeze.

"Yeah, that's what I thought. You scared to shoot the ball." Slim told Freeze, as he egged Freeze on.

"Look, l will even give you some room," Slim yelled out to Freeze after he stepped back a few steps from Freeze.

"Show me what ya' working wit', playa," Slim said to Freeze, as he challenged Freeze again.

Freeze squared up to shoot the ball.

"N-O-O!" JJ yelled out to Freeze, as the ball flew out of Freeze's hands.

It appeared the ball was moving in slow motion as it made its way to the hoop. As the ball reached the hoop, it appeared to go halfway into the hoop and it then popped out of the basket.

Big Baby grabbed the rebound over a shorter JJ. He cleared the key and he quickly turned back towards the basket and slammed dunked the ball over JJ.

"Game over," Slim yelled to them, as he did his victory dance, making his hands like guns shooting in the air.

He walked over to pick up the pile of $20s sitting at the foot of the basketball pole that was weighed down by JJ's T-shirt.

Freeze walked towards Slim in an aggressive manner with his fists balled up.

"Man, you hustled us." Freeze protested to Slim.

"Don't be mad, bro'. That thar' is part of the game." Slim told Freeze, with a big smile on his face, as he picked up the twenties off of the ground.

Freeze cornered Slim at the basketball ball pole and hemmed him up by the collar of his shirt.

"C'mon, man. We won fair and square." Slim pleaded with Freeze, as he stood there with his hands up in the air.

"Hey, homie. Be cool." JJ said to Freeze, as he interceded with Freeze and Slim before the incident got out of hand.

"C'mon, it ain't worth it, bruh'," JJ told Freeze, as he pulled Freeze back from Slim.

Slim straightened out his collar and began distributing the funds he had won with Big Baby.

After he gave Big Baby his share of the money, Freeze went back to Freeze and handed him $20 and he said to Freeze, in his smooth voice, "No bad feelings, my brother."

Freeze snatched the $20 bill out of Slim's hand, balled it up, and threw it into the middle of the court.

Slim backed away from Freeze with both hands up in the air in a conciliatory manner and he turned towards JJ with his hand extended to shake JJ's hand.

He said to JJ, "You gotta' do something 'bout' that temper of yo' boi'."

Slim stood there with his hand extended for a few seconds, as JJ stood there staring him down, with his arms folded. He refused to shake Slim's hand.

Slim slowly withdrew his hand from JJ. He motioned his hand back across his wavy hair and he told JJ, as he walked away laughing, looking over his shoulder, tauntingly he said to him, "Hey potna' dude. Don't go away mad. Just go away."

Big Baby counted his share of the winnings. He then came over and shook JJ's hand.

"Good game, bro." He said to JJ, as the two embraced each other.

Big Baby went over to shake Freeze's hand.

He said to him, "Good game, homie."

Freeze, still steaming mad from having lost the game, didn't respond to Big Baby.

Big Baby held his hand out for a few seconds, waiting for Freeze to shake his hand.

After Freeze refused to shake his hand, Big Baby patted Freeze on the shoulder and walked away.

Both JJ and Freeze just stood there on the basketball court for a few minutes in silence. Finally, JJ spoke.

"You ought not to treat Big Baby like that. He's a cool dude." JJ told Freeze.

"I know. I was just mad at that asshole, Slim." Freeze told JJ.

Another moment of silence went by. JJ broke the silence again.

"Now we broke," JJ complained to Freeze.

"Man, we should off took them," Freeze told JJ.

"Yeah, if you would have passed me the ball," JJ told Freeze.

"Oh, it's my fault. Whatever happened to we win as a team, we lose as a team?" Freeze asked JJ.

There was another moment of silence, which was broken by JJ again.

"Yeah, you right, homie. No finger-pointing." JJ said to Freeze.

Again, there was a moment of silence, as the only sound that could be heard was the traffic going by on the nearby street. Freeze broke the silence this time.

"Yeah, you right. It was my fault. I should've passed it. I let my pride get to me." Freeze was admitted to JJ.

"That's okay," JJ responded to him.

Freeze told JJ, "We will get them next time. You noticed this is the closest we came to beating them in a long time." Freeze pointed out to JJ.

Freeze added, "Yeah, we getting better, huh?

"Yeah, we are," JJ told Freeze.

JJ then said to him, "C'mon, I will treat you to lunch."

"Ha, with what? We both broke." Freeze told JJ.

There was another moment of silence. They both then simultaneously looked towards the middle of the court where the balled-up $20 bill still lay.

Both of them jumped up and raced towards it. They both dived for it at the same time and ended up lying sprawled out on the basketball court.

JJ reached it first. They both sat up and started laughing.

"Getting slow in your old age, huh old man?" JJ said to Freeze.

"Ok, you win. I am at your mercy." Freeze told JJ.

"How bout we split it," JJ told Freeze.

"We ride together," Freeze said to JJ.

"We die together," JJ said to Freeze.

And they both said to each other in unison, "I am my brother's keeper."

They do a funny handshake with each other and the two of them set off from the park passing the basketball back and forth to each other, taking turns dribbling the basketball as they headed on their way to the burger place.

CHAPTER 3 THE PRANK

JJ was up early Monday morning. For most kids, the first day of school was a drag.

However, for a jock, especially a senior jock, you didn't mind the first day of school, because you were treated like royalty at school.

"Good morning, son. You up early this morning. See you got those clothes on I bought you." His mother said to him, as JJ came down the stairs.

"C'mon stand here so I can check you out." She said to him, as he stood there yawning.

"C'mon, Ma," JJ complained to her as she fixed his collar.

"Now, you know Momma gotta' make sure you looking proper, baby, for your first day as a senior." She said to him.

"C'mon, Ma, I am not a baby no mo'." He told her.

"Hush, boy." She said as she was primping his clothes and fixing his collar, as he made faces and grunts of disapproval.

After she was done making a fuss over him, she stood back and said to him, "Now you gonna always be my baby, son. You hear me?"

"Yeah, Ma." He said to her under his breath.

"You need a ride to school?" She asked him as she offered him a ride with a big grin on her face.

"No, Ma, yo' lil baby can walk." He told her sarcastically, in a baby voice.

He added, "Ma, I am starting my senior year in high school. Not kindergarten." He pointed out to her.

"Okay, baby. Give Mama a kiss." She said to him.

He gave his mother a peck on the cheek. He then was off to school.

He walked briskly away from the house until he was out of sight of his mother.

He then quickly took off the clothing his mother had bought for him, revealing the beige Dickey pants and red Polo shirt he had on under the clothes he was wearing.

He stuffed the clothes he had on that his mother had provided for him into his backpack. After he switched clothes, he scurried off to school.

When he got on campus, he noticed a crowd gathered at the Quad in the middle of the campus. There was a lot of joking around and laughter going on.

As he approached the crowd, he saw amongst the crowd laughing harder than anyone, was Freeze.

"What's so funny?" He inquired of his friend, Freeze, as he approached him.

Freeze answered him and he said to him, "Wssup', dude." He stammered out between his laughter.

He greeted JJ with a high five, and he said to him, "You late, dude."

"Late for what?" JJ asked Freeze.

"You missed out on all the fun, look," Freeze said to JJ, as he pointed towards the flagpole in the right corner of the Quad.

JJ looked up at the flagpole. There, hanging from the flagpole, was a human body. It was the pale, weird-looking kid.

"Momma!" The weird kid yelled out.

"Momma!" The crowd yelled out mocking him.

"Ain't that the funniest thing you ever seen?" Freeze proclaimed to JJ.

"Yeah, the funniest thing," JJ repeated after Freeze halfheartedly, because he was not really feeling this joke.

"Momma!" The boy yelled out again.

His underwear showed as the hook from the flagpole rope bungled his blue underwear into a wedgie. His pants were down to his ankles now and his shirt was covering his pale face.

"Momma!" The boy yelled out again.

This time the rope had rotated his body to face the crowd. His shirt had fallen to the ground. You could see the tears streaming down from the boy's face.

Somehow, JJ did not see the humor in this prank anymore.

He turned towards Freeze and he said to him, "Ok, Freeze. That's enough. Let him down." JJ insisted upon Freeze to do.

"Momma!" The poor boy moaned again.

By this time, a mob had gathered around and some of the most raucous people had started pelting objects at the boy.

"You want him down, dude? Let him down yourself." Freeze said to JJ, as he pelted the boy with some of the wood chips that underlined the trees on campus.

JJ stood there a minute in silence, watching the crowd taunt the boy. Everything seemed to be happening in slow motion, as JJ stood there pondering on whether he was going to untie the rope and let the poor kid down or not.

"Momma!" The boy called out again.

Hearing his last cry out for help, JJ decided to take action.

"OK, I will let him down," JJ told Freeze, as he moved towards the rope bound to the flagpole.

The crowd began to, "Boo," as JJ began to untie the rope.

"Hater!" Someone yelled out to him, as JJ slowly took the knot out of the rope.

First, the crowd was in a big uproar. There then came a sudden hush.

JJ was so intrigued in getting the knot out of the rope, that he did not notice the person that came up behind him.

A hand came from behind him and landed on his shoulder.

JJ shrugged the hand off of his shoulder without looking behind him. Again, the hand came upon his shoulder.

"No, enough is enough," JJ said in response to the hand that had been placed upon his shoulder. The hand patted him on the shoulder again.

"I'm not trying to hear you," JJ responded to the hand, as he continued to work on the knot in the rope.

This time the person behind him turned him around. To his surprise, he was now facing Mr. Jackson. He took a big swallow. It felt like his heart had fallen down to the bottom of his feet.

"I-I -I- d-d." He stammered, trying to deny any guilt.

"To my office." A strict-faced Mr. Jackson said to him, as he pointed his huge hand towards the office.

JJ trudged slowly to the office.

"Get him down!" Mr. Jackson ordered the mob to do so in his big booming voice.

About five people seemed to rush over to get the boy down upon Mr. Jackson's command.

Mr. Jackson was an imposing man. He stood about six feet four and weighed a solid two hundred fifty pounds, but at that time, to JJ, he appeared to be an eight-foot-tall monster.

JJ arrived at the office door and he waited for Mr. Jackson to open the door for him.

"Have a seat, boy." Mr. Jackson commanded him to do, with authority in his voice.

You could tell when Mr. Jackson was angry with you. Not by his rough mannerisms, but by how he addressed you. If you were addressed as a son or as a young man, chances were you were in his good graces.

But if you were addressed as, "boy", chances were you were in deep trouble.

Mr. Jackson called over the intercom to Miss Summers.

"Bring the suspension papers, please." He said to her.

JJ sunk down in his chair. Miss Summers brought over some papers from the main office and gave them to Mr. Jackson. Mr. Jackson sat there filling out the papers.

When he was done filling out the papers, he handed a copy of the papers to JJ and he told him, "OK, boy. Take these papers home and have your mother sign them. She and I will have a conference, soon."

JJ took the papers from Mr. Jackson. He grabbed his book bag, walked out of the office, and started walking to the bus stop.

It took forever, it seemed, to get to the bus stop. He got there just as a bus was leaving. He tried to flag it down, but it was too late. The bus had already pulled off without him. He dropped his book bag at his feet.

"Man, this has been some day." He thought to himself.

"What else could go wrong?" He asked himself.

Just then, five-o pulled up.

"Great," JJ said, as the officer pulled up in front of him and stepped out of his car.

As the officer approached JJ, JJ put his hands up in the air above his head.

"Son, you've been watching too much TV. Put your hands down." The officer told JJ.

JJ slowly put his hands down.

The officer was a tall, White guy. He was clean-shaven, with average height and weight. Looked to be in his late 20s or early 30s.

JJ asked him, "How are you doing, Officer?"

"I'm doing mighty fine, young man." The officer responded to JJ.

"Little early to be out of school?" The officer asked JJ.

JJ began to reach into his book bag. He then stopped and looked at the gun on the officer's holster.

"I have papers in my book bag," JJ told the officer.

The officer nodded his approval for JJ to go into his book bag.

JJ reached into his book bag and pulled out his suspension papers. He handed the papers over to the officer.

The officer looked over the papers. After he looked over the papers, the officer handed the papers back to JJ.

"First day of school and suspended, huh, son?" The officer said to JJ.

Yeah, officer, but I'm a good kid." JJ told the officer.

"Yeah, I know, kid. Let me guess. You didn't do it?" The officer asked JJ, anticipating JJ's excuse.

"Really, Officer. I really didn't do it." JJ insisted.

"You know how many times I hear that story, son?" The officer asked JJ.

"Probably a million times, Officer, but I am the one outta' one million who is telling you the truth," JJ told the officer.

The officer looked straight at JJ, and he said to him, "Somehow, I believe you, son. I've been there where you are. I know it may seem tough now, but you'll get over it."

"Really, you mean you've been suspended before?" JJ asked the officer.

"Of course, I have. I haven't been wearing a badge all of my life." The officer told JJ.

"What were you suspended for?" JJ asked the officer.

"I'm not going to go into any detail, but let's just say it had to do with some girls." The officer told JJ.

The officer then looked at JJ and asked him, "Did your situation have to do with some girls?"

JJ shook his head from side to side to indicate, "No".

Now the officer shook his head and he told JJ, "See, son, if you gonna' get into trouble. You got to be smart about it. My suspension was almost worth it." The officer told JJ with a big grin on his face.

JJ laughed at him.

"You have a good day, son." The officer told JJ.

"Goodbye, officer," JJ said to the officer.

The officer got back into his car and drove off, as JJ sat at the bus stop waiting for the bus, pondering his dilemma.

"First day of school and suspended. Got to get home and erase those messages on the phone before Mom gets home." JJ thought to himself, as he waited on the bus.

"You riding, young man?" A deep hoarse voice called out to him.

JJ was so caught up in his thoughts, that he did not notice the bus pull up.

He looked up to see a heavyset, bearded, White man, sporting his khaki brown uniform, speaking to him.

"You riding or what, Buddy? I got a schedule to keep, now. Ain't got all day." He told JJ.

JJ slowly got up and he stepped onto the bus. He showed the bus driver his bus pass and got on the bus and he went to the back of the bus.

About five minutes into the bus ride, the bus driver called back to JJ.

"Suspended from school, huh?" The driver asked JJ.

JJ looked surprised.

"What was it with these old people? They psychic or what?" JJ asked himself, trying to figure out how the driver knew that he had been suspended from school.

JJ answered the bus driver and he said to him, "Yes, sir, but I didn't do it."

The driver told JJ, "Yes, young man. That's everybody's story. That was my story when I got suspended from school." He told JJ.

"You got suspended from school?" JJ asked the driver.

"Yes, I got suspended from school, young man." The driver answered JJ.

"Wow, first a police officer and now a bus driver," JJ said to himself.

JJ was beginning to think that getting suspended from school was some type of rite of passage.

"What did you get suspended for?" JJ asked the bus driver.

"My crime was graffiti." The driver told JJ.

The two were quiet for a few minutes.

The bus driver then asked JJ, "Answer me this question. The incident that happened. Could you have prevented it from happening?"

JJ thought about the question the driver had asked him for a moment.

Finally, JJ answered him and he said to him, "Yes, I probably could have."

The bus driver said to JJ, "Well, son. That makes you as guilty as the perpetrator."

JJ sat quietly and thought about what the driver had said to him.

"I want you to sit back and marinate on that for the rest of the bus ride." The driver told JJ.

Each moment that passed by, JJ tried to think of an alibi to tell his mother why he had been suspended from school. On what seemed like a forever bus trip, he finally reached his stop.

"I'm getting off here, sir," JJ told the bus driver.

JJ took a deep breath as he exited the bus.

"You have a nice day, young man." The bus driver told JJ, as JJ got off the bus.

"Keep your head up." He added, trying to encourage JJ.

"Thank you, sir," JJ told him, as he got off of the bus.

JJ stood there and watched the bus till it was out of sight. After he couldn't see the bus any longer, he slowly turned and walked meticulously down the street towards his home.

Like a convicted man walking towards the gallows, he started to walk down the street. As he neared his home, he could see a woman in a blue dress, with a red headscarf tied around her hair on the porch of his house. She stood on the porch with her arms folded.

"Too late to erase the messages. She already knows." He thought to himself, as he neared his home.

As he got closer to the house, he could see the fire in his mother's eyes and the serious scowl on her face.

He walked up to the porch and he looked into his mother's face. The expression on her face did not change. She did not say a word. She just pointed towards the front door, motioning for him to enter the house. He entered the house slowly.

When he got inside, he waited in the corridor for his mother to come in. She stood motionless on the porch for about five minutes. She then slowly entered the house.

Again, without saying a word, she motioned for JJ to go sit on the couch.

JJ removed his book bag and set it on the floor. He then sat down slowly on the couch.

His mother sat down on the couch on the opposite side of the room. She sat silently, staring into space. Again, she remained silent.

The tension in the air was thicker than mud on a cold Winter's night. The silence was almost deafening. Finally, JJ decided to break the silence.

"But, Ma. I did..." Before he could finish his sentence, she had put her hand up to halt his speech. Again, there was silence in the room.

After about another five minutes of silence, she spoke.

"Hand me that cell phone." She ordered him to do.

He went into his backpack to grab his phone. As he was getting his phone out of his book bag, he tried to plea his case to her again

"But, Ma..." He started to say to her.

This time she put her finger in front of her mouth, cutting his conversation short again, as she shook her head back and forth.

She motioned for him to hand over his cell phone. He handed it over to her.

"Now, go to your room. I don't want to see you anymore today." She told him.

He slowly began to ascend the stairs to his room.

She added, "And take that video game out of your room."

He turned around on the stairs and he said to her, "C'mon, Ma."

"Don't c'mon Ma me, boy." She said to him, as she pointed her finger upwards for him to go upstairs to his room.

"And no dinner for you tonight." She informed him.

He huffed as he stomped up the rest of the stairs to his room. He entered his room and he plopped down on his bed.

"Video game!" He heard his mother's voice ring out from downstairs.

He looked towards the TV in the corner of his room. He stormed towards the TV and snatched the video game console off of the top of the TV.

Begrudgingly, he unplugged it, stormed towards the entrance of his bedroom, and laid the game outside of his bedroom door.

He then stomped back to his bed and plopped down on it.

"You need to get rid of that attitude, boy!" His mother yelled out up the stairs to him.

He took a deep breath and sighed.

"You hear me, boy. Don't let me have to come up there." She told him, as she threatened to come up the stairs.

"Alright, Ma." He answered her.

"And no dinner for you tonight." She repeated to him.

"OK, Ma, I got it. No dinner for me. I'm gonna starve like a Third World kid." He said to her.

He sat at the end of his bed, staring at the wall. Out of the corner of his eye, he spotted a magazine. He got up off of his bed to grab the magazine off of the floor.

He called downstairs to his mother and he sarcastically said to her, with a smirk on his face, "Can I read a magazine?"

His mother answered him and she said to him,

"Jonathan Jeffries Jenkins, don't you get smart with me, boy! Do you want me to come up there?" She yelled at him, threatening to come up the stairs

"Uh oh, this was serious." He said to himself.

She called him by all three of his names. The last time she did that she almost blew a gasket.

"You hear me, boy? You want me to come up these stairs!" She yelled out to him again, as she began to come up the stairs.

"No, Ma, it's cool. Please, don't come upstairs, Ma." He pled with her not to do so.

He heard her stop, turn around, and go back downstairs.

"Whew, that was close." He said to himself, as he heard her say to herself, "Don't play with me, boy. I brought you into this world and I'll take you out."

He picked up a magazine with a guy dressed in a basketball uniform, holding a basketball in his hands.

He grabbed the magazine and laid down on his belly on his bed. He began thumbing through the magazine.

"Now that's going to be me." He said pointing to one of the players in the magazine, with a big smile on his face.

"NBA bound." He bragged to himself.

He continued to thumb through the magazine until he fell asleep.

He was awakened about three hours later by a gentle voice calling his name.

"JJ, wake up, baby." The voice said to him.

First, he thought he was dreaming. He sat up straight on the bed and rubbed the sleep out of his eyes.

As his eyes began to focus. A brown skin woman began to appear before him. She held a tray of food with a glass of milk on it.

"Here, baby. Momma got you some spaghetti." She told him.

He blinked his eyes once more. He then grabbed the tray from her, which had a plate of spaghetti and a glass of milk on it.

His mother turned and exited the room. He had lost count of the times his mother had sent him to bed without dinner, only to bring him something to eat later on in the night.

"Say your blessing, baby." She told him, as she descended the stairs.

"Yeah, Ma." He answered her.

He said a quick blessing. He then began chowing down on the food on his plate. After he ate his food, he fell back asleep.

CHAPTER 4 JJ'S PUNISHMENT

"Jay-Jay." A drowsy JJ heard his mother's voice call his name as she shook him out of a deep sleep.

"Get up, boy." She commanded him to do, as she was still shaking him vigorously.

"Alright, Ma. I'm up. Stop shaking me, please." He replied as he sat up on the edge of his bed.

"Boy, don't you sass me?" She said to him, as she gave him a quick slap upside his head.

"Ow, Ma. Dang, sorry. I said please." He told her, as he rubbed his head.

"Oh, you gonna' be sorry. Here I am missing half a day's work because you acting foolish at school." She told him.

"Ma, I tried to tell you. It wasn't me." JJ told her.

"What you say, boy? You talking back again?" She asked him as she walked towards him with her hand raised, as she was ready to strike him again.

"No, Ma, I'm not talking back." He said to her, as he put his hands up to protect his face.

"Please, Ma, put your 45s back in their holster." He told her, referring to her raised hand that was readying to strike him again.

She stepped away from him and she continued to rant and rave at him as she left the room.

JJ got up and went to the bathroom. He did a quick wash-up and brushed his teeth. All the while, he could hear his mother fussing about losing a day's work.

He paid little attention to her rambling on. He had other things on his mind. Right now, his mind was concentrated on going to the principal's office.

"Two weeks suspension. I can live with that." He thought to himself.

After all, it was only September. Basketball season didn't start till November.

It was the second consequence that worried him the most.

"Getting kicked off of the basketball team." He thought to himself.

He finished brushing his teeth and he then stepped into his bedroom. He laid his clothes out on the bed. Just as he got undressed out of his PJs, his mother came busting through the door.

"Boy, you need to hurry up here and stop taking your time." She told JJ.

JJ stood up and covered his unclad body with the clothes he had laid out on the bed.

"Ma, I don't have any clothes on." He told her, as he stood there naked as a newborn babe.

His mother crossed her arms and looked over the rim of her glasses and she said to him, "Boy, you ain't got anything I ain't' seen and nothing I want to see. Now get your clothes on and let's go." She told him.

"Alright, Ma. Give me some privacy, please." He requested of her.

He then jokingly added, "Lil JJ, not Lil JJ anymore. There've been some alterations down there since you last changed my diaper." He said to her with a smirk on his face.

His mother smacked him upside the head, again.

"Ow, Ma!" He said to her in reaction to her popping him upside the head.

"Boy, don't you joke with me at a time like this?" She told him.

"Alright, alright, Ma. Sorry, be cool with that right hook of yours." He said rubbing the left side of his head.

He added, "Man, you ought to get that right hook of yours registered." He said to her.

"Are you still joking around?" She asked him with a stern voice.

"No, ma'am." He said to her, as he straightened up his face and took the smile off of his face, as he tried to look serious.

"I'm getting dressed now." He told her.

His mother stepped out of the room. She was still talking to herself.

JJ finished getting dressed. After he combed his hair, he threw on some deodorant and headed downstairs. His mother met him at the foot of the stairs.

"Here is a breakfast sandwich for you." She said to him, as she handed him a sandwich and a cup of juice.

"You can eat it in the car." She told him.

"Man, this really must've been serious. She was letting him eat in the car. That was like her letting him cuss in church. That like, never happened." He said to himself

He and his mother exited the house towards a red Volvo parked in the driveway. From there they were off to his school.

From the time they left the house, till the time they got into the car, his mother was fussing about everything from JJ shaming the family, to JJ getting suspended from school to JJ not taking the trash out the previous night.

Everything she said went over his head. The only thing he could think of was if he was going to get kicked off of the football and basketball teams.

"Get out of the car, boy!" His mother screamed at him, as they had arrived at the school parking lot.

He was so caught up in his thoughts that he did not realize that they had pulled up in front of the school.

JJ slowly got out of the car. His mother sat in the driver's seat waiting for him to open the car door for her. He ran around from the passenger's side of the car to the driver's side of the car to open her car door. Once she was out of the car the two of them walked towards the school office.

The walk from the parking lot to the principal's office was like a walk through a graveyard at night, with a full moon shining.

Finally, the tedious trek to the principal's office ended. JJ and his mother stood at the office door.

"Uh-hum." His mom made a sound that was intended as a hint for him to open the door for her.

JJ opened the door for his mother. As they stepped into the office. They came face to face with Miss Summers. One of the school secretaries. She greeted them.

"Good morning, Miss Jenkins." Miss Summers said to his mother.

JJ's mother said nothing to her. She just nodded her head.

"Mr. Johnson will be with you shortly." Miss Summers informed the two of them.

Both JJ and his mother took a seat in the main office. His mother grabbed a magazine that was on the table and she started reading it.

After they had waited for about ten minutes, Mr. Johnson entered the main office.

He walked over to the secretary and asked her, "You got any mail for me, Miss Summers?"

She handed him some papers. She then whispered something into his ear, as she pointed towards JJ and his mother.

Principal Johnson looked over at them and he walked over to the two of them and he introduced himself.

"Hello, ma'am. I am Mr. Johnson. Could you step into my office, please?" He asked them as he led them to his office.

"Have a seat." He told them, as he directed them over to two chairs in front of his desk.

"Now, Mr. Jenkins. What do you have to say for yourself?" He asked JJ.

JJ went on to explain to him how he had walked upon the scene and that actually, he was helping the boy. Not hazing him.

"Well, Mr. Jenkins, the vice-principal said different." Principal Johnson said to him, contradicting JJ's version of the events that took place.

"Miss Jenkins, do you have anything to say about the situation?" Mr. Johnson asked her.

"Well, sir, when I first heard about this. I was highly upset with my son, but after I heard my son's side of the story. I believe him. My son does not lie to me and he is a good kid." She added.

JJ sat up proudly in his seat. That was the first time he had heard his mother talk about him in such a manner.

"Well, unfortunately, Miss Jenkins. Our vice principal says different. We frown upon this type of behavior at this school. Hazing is a very serious offense. I have no other choice, but to suspend your son for two weeks." Mr. Johnson informed her.

"Well, at least I am still on the football and basketball teams." JJ thought to himself.

At that moment, Mr. Jackson stepped into the office.

He looked towards JJ and his mother and he said to them, "So, this is the young man with the hazing incident, huh? What are the consequences of his behavior?" Mr. Jackson inquired of Mr. Johnson.

"Two weeks suspended." Mr. Johnson informed Mr. Jackson.

"Oh, no, that's just a slap on the wrist. Last year we expelled a couple of students for this kind of behavior." Mr. Jackson informed them.

He then asked them, "Isn't he (JJ) on the football and basketball teams?"

Everyone in the room nodded their heads. JJ gulped and took a deep breath in anticipation of the next words coming out of Mr. Jackson's mouth.

"Well, I think he ought to be kicked off of both teams." Mr. Jackson insisted that he do.

JJ felt like a dagger had been thrust through his heart.

"Damn, off of the football and basketball teams. That was like the only purpose for coming to school." JJ said to himself.

"Man, I wonder if I am off of the baseball team, too?" He wondered.

He then thought about it and he said to himself, "I dare not ask them. Don't want to put any ideas into their heads. I will cross that river when we get to it."

First, JJ sank down disappointingly in his seat. He then heard the voice of his coach, Mr. Smith, saying in his head, "Never show your opponent your weakness."

At hearing those words in his head, JJ quickly sat up in his seat. He tried to look cool, but inside, he was devastated. It took all of his bravado to keep him from crying.

"Now, Mr. Jackson, my son was counting on getting a basketball scholarship to get into college." His mother informed the vice principal.

JJ thought, "If there was a silver lining in this situation, it was hearing his mother sticking up for him."

"Well, Miss. Jenkins. I have to agree with Mr. Jackson. Our student-athletes have to be role models in this school. So, as of now, Mr. Jenkins, you are suspended from the football and basketball teams." Mr. Johnson told him.

JJ thought, "Wow, why not just give me the electric chair."

Miss Jenkins stood up abruptly and she said to Mr. Johnson, "I think this is so unfair. Come on, JJ." She told him as she summoned JJ to leave with her.

As she exited the office, she turned back towards Mr. Johnson and she said to him sharply, "This is not the last you will see of me!"

The both of them, JJ and his mother, headed for the parking lot. JJ's mom was fuming mad over the situation at hand. She was talking to herself, as she usually does when she is upset.

"This time, at least, she's not mad at me." JJ thought to himself.

When they arrived at the car. His mother stood in the car waiting for JJ to open her door for her.

"Uh-hum." She said to him, as she gave JJ a hint to open the car door for her.

JJ ran around from the passenger door to the driver's side door and opened the door for his mother. He then went and sat down in the front passenger side of the car. They both sat in the car for a moment in silence. JJ spoke first.

"Thanks, Ma." He told his mother.

She looked at him with a puzzled look and asked him, "Thanks, for what, son?"

"Thanks, for believing in me," JJ told her.

"Oh, baby. You don't have to thank me for doing the right thing. One thing I know is my baby don't lie to me." She told him.

There was a moment of silence.

His mother then said to him, "Except that time you stole those cupcakes out of the cupboard."

They looked at each other and they both started laughing.

"Ma, I was only four years old then." He informed her.

"I know baby." She said to him.

She then added, "Standing there with cupcakes all over your face. Denying you had taken the cupcakes."

They both laughed again.

As their laughter subsided, JJ looked at his mom and said to her, "Seeing you in action today at my school was worth getting those two right hooks upside my head."

"Oh, I'm sorry, baby. I just want the best for you. Mama didn't hurt you, did she?" She asked him.

"Naw', Ma, you know it takes more than that to get through that thick skull of mine." He told her.

They sat back and laughed again. After the laughter subsided, they sat there quietly for a minute. JJ broke the silence again.

JJ said to his mother, pointing to his left cheek, "Give me a wet one, right here."

His mother looked at him in surprise and she asked him, "Oh, you mean it's not embarrassing for Momma to give her boy a kiss in public?"

"Naw, Ma, give it up to yo' lil Pookie. Some love." He told her, as he pointed to his cheek and he encouraged her to give him a kiss on the cheek.

His mother laid a kiss on his cheek.

"Love ya, Ma." He told her.

"Love ya, son." She responded to him.

They both just sat in the car for a few moments. Just enjoying each other's company.

CHAPTER 5 JJ'S REDEMPTION

Usually, two weeks out of school would be like a vacation, but, instead, these two weeks were like being incarcerated.

There was no sneaking out of the house, with nosy Miss Harris on one side of their house and nosy Mama Jewel on the other side.

"Damn, do they ever sleep?" JJ thought to himself.

However, his mother concluded that JJ did no wrong. She still did not want him in the streets all day.

"Too much trouble out there." She would say to him.

It wasn't a total loss, though. Momma did allow JJ to have his TV and video games back. So that made the two weeks go by a little faster.

Now it was Monday morning. Two weeks had gone by. First day back to school. Finally, bailing out of this prison, or so it seemed. Back to school today. Nothing to look forward to, though.

"No football, no basketball, no scholarship." He reminded himself

"Damn, all because I'm trying to do a good deed. Never again." JJ thought to himself.

"No more Mr. Nice Guy." He proclaimed.

He got up slowly and went through his usual daily routine. He sat up on his bed, clad in his white boxer underwear. He sat there for about five minutes, gathering his thoughts. He then let out a big yawn and took a long stretch.

"Hmm, where is Ma? She would usually be up here by now. Bugging me to get up." He thought to himself.

"Ma." He called out for her.

She did not answer.

"Mama." He yelled out again.

Still, there was no answer.

He slowly got up. He started his morning routine. He laid his clothes out on his bed. He then went to take a quick wash off and he brushed his teeth. After he finished washing up, he went back to his room and got dressed.

"Mama." He called out her name once again.

There was no answer. He began to search the house from room to room, trying to find her.

"Mama." He called out for her again.

Still, there was no answer. He went downstairs. He looked into the kitchen. In the kitchen, there was a note on the kitchen table. He picked it up and read it. It was in his mother's handwriting.

The note read, "Left your breakfast in the microwave oven. Love, Ma."

He looked into the microwave oven. There sat a green plate with some scrambled eggs and some finger sausages on it. He warmed the plate up in the microwave and he took a bottle of orange juice out of the refrigerator, as his food warmed up.

He looked for a cup in the cupboard, but he couldn't find one. He began drinking the orange juice out of the bottle.

"Ding." The microwave bell went off.

He retrieved his plate from the microwave. He almost dropped the plate because it was so hot. He didn't bother to sit down or get eating utensils. He began chowing down his food using his hands. He chased down the food with what was left in the bottle of OJ. He then gathered his book bag and left out the door. He was off, on his way to school.

He decided to walk to school instead of riding the bus. The long walk would do a lot to refresh his mind.

The trek to school was a tedious journey. The whole time he walked, he pondered on how boring it was going to be without football and basketball this year.

He finally made it to school. He plodded up the stairs of the front of the building. He didn't notice the other students buzzing around him. He barely saw the person walking up from behind him.

"Mr. Jenkins." A voice from behind him called out his name.

He jumped, as he was startled by the person that had come up from behind him.

He turned to face a short, stocky, pale-faced, blonde-haired man. He was about five feet tall and five feet wide. It looked like he was more of a court jester the way he was dressed in a polka dot shirt and bright red pants and the toes of his red shoes appeared to curl up to the sky.

He looked so round It looked like you could just roll him down the hallway. It was Mr. Garrett, the hall monitor.

"Mr. Jenkins." He said again in his deep baritone voice.

"Yeah, Mr. Garret," JJ answered him.

"You are wanted in the office, son." Mr. Garrett informed JJ, as he pointed down the hall with his fat stubby index finger.

"Yes, sir," JJ answered him

JJ looked down the hallway and he stared for about a minute. Finally, he plodded down the hallway toward the principal's office.

"What now?" He thought to himself.

He had been in the principal's office more times this month than all of his entire high school stay.

He entered the office. Ms. Mills, one of the school secretaries, greeted him.

"Good morning, Mr. Jenkins." She said to him in her sultry Southern drawl.

"Have a seat till Mr. Johnson calls for you, baby." She told him.

Ms. Mills was a petite little lady. Every boy in school wanted to get a look at Ms. Mills in the front office.

She was stacked like hotcakes on an early Sunday morning breakfast platter. She was always walking around in those short sexy skirts, showing off her fine body, in her low low-cut blouses. She showed off more cleavage than the bedrock of a mountaintop rock quarry.

So, there she was. Flaunting herself around the office with her halter top and her mini skirt. For a minute, JJ was so entrenched in watching her, he had forgotten what he had come to the office for.

JJ heard a door close behind him, which snapped him back to reality. He looked towards Mr. Johnson's office and he strained to see through the glass that was lined with wires.

As he looked through the office window, he made out Mr. Johnson, his mother, Coach Smith, the goofy kid, and the goofy kid's mother. They were all in Mr. Johnson's office.

JJ thought to himself, "What's my mother doing here? I thought she was at work."

He then thought, "What now?"

He took a deep breath and sighed. JJ sat there twiddling his thumbs and fidgeting around. He anxiously awaited to see what was going on in Mr. Johnson's office.

"Mr. Jenkins, enter my office please." Mr. Johnson, finally, came out of his office and called for him.

JJ entered Mr. Johnson's office. He stood at the office door and looked around at everyone in the office. It appeared all eyes were on him.

"Have a seat, Mr. Jenkins." Mr. Johnson told him.

JJ came into the office and he had a seat. He sat in a chair next to his mother.

He looked up to meet the eyes of the mother of the weird kid. It appeared her eyes were piercing his soul. Mr. Johnson started off the conversation.

"Well, Mr. Jenkins. We are here to discuss your status at this school." Mr. Johnson told him.

JJ looked at his mother, whose arms were folded, and her stare was stern. JJ did not have a clue as to what was going on.

"So, first we have agreed among us, that you owe Mr. Swisher and his mother an apology." Mr. Johnson told him.

"Bu-t." JJ started to say, but his mother interrupted him by making a throat sound.

"Uh-hum." His mother said to him as she cut him off from saying what he was about to say. She flashed that deadly stare of hers at him.

JJ took a deep breath and sighed. He turned to the funny-looking boy and his mother. He sighed one more time. He then addressed the weird kid and his mother.

Miss –." JJ paused because he just realized, he did not know the lady's name.

He looked at the principal seeking an answer.

"Miss Swisher." The principal said to him, filling in the blank.

"Miss. Swisher and uh,–" Again JJ paused and looked at the principal because he did not know the weird kid's name either.

"And Benjamin." Mr. Johnson said to JJ. Once more filling in the blank.

"And Benjamin, I apologize for my behavior," JJ said to both of them.

"And it won't happen again." JJ's mother added.

JJ looked at his mother. She gave him that iron stare of hers.

He turned back to the two of them (Benjamin and his mother) and he added, "And it won't happen again."

"You ought to be ashamed of yourself." The boy's mother exclaimed as she pointed her skinny finger towards him.

"Yes, ma'am," JJ replied to her sheepishly.

"Miss Swisher, could you leave us alone now?" Mr. Johnson requested her to do.

The lady grabbed the funny-looking boy by the hand and they exited the office. As she exited the office, she looked back at JJ and she rolled her eyes at him.

"Now for you, Mr. Jenkins. Your mother and I and Coach Smith have worked out a deal so that you can still play basketball."

JJ looked at Coach Smith and Coach Smith nodded his head at him.

Mr. Johnson asked JJ, "You still want to play football and basketball, don't you?"

"Why, yes sir." JJ eagerly said as he perked up in his seat.

"You, Mr. Jenkins, can play football and basketball on one condition." Mr. Johnson told JJ.

"Yes, sir. Anything, sir." JJ eagerly said to Mr. Johnson.

Mr. Johnson said to JJ, "The condition is that you show Benjamin around campus his first month here."

JJ was taken aback at what Mr. Johnson had just requested that he do. This was the last thing he was expected to be made to be. A chaperone for the kid he was accused of bullying.

"Show Benjamin around campus for a month?" JJ asked Mr. Johnson, as he repeated what Mr. Johnson had requested of him to do.

"Yes, he is new to this environment and he needs someone of your stature and influence to guide him around. This way you will only be suspended two football games and when the basketball season starts, you will be able to start every game of basketball. Pending you don't get into any more trouble." Mr. Johnson told JJ.

JJ looked at his mother with a puzzled look on his face.

She responded to the way he looked at her and she said to him, forcefully, "You heard what the man said. You have to show Benjamin around for a month. Thank the man." She added for him to do.

JJ took a deep breath and said to Mr. Johnson, "Thank you, Mr. Johnson."

"Well, if the both of you have no other questions, I believe we are done here." Mr. Johnson told them.

"Thank you, Mr. Johnson." JJ's mother said to him.

"Thank you and your son." Mr. Johnson responded back to her.

JJ's mother stared at him. She then gave him the evil eye until he finally got the hint.

"Oh, thank you, Mr. Johnson," JJ added in a dry tone.

JJ got up and slowly left the office with his mother. She gave him a quick peck on the cheek and she was on her way off to work.

As JJ left and exited the office, he saw a ruckus over on the south side of the school campus, near the basketball courts. As he got closer to the courts, he noticed Freeze throwing something. There was a crowd cheering him on. In the middle of the crowd stood Benjamin. Freeze was hitting him with water balloons.

Each time a balloon hit Benjamin, the crowd would cheer. JJ walked up behind Freeze as he reared back to throw another balloon. JJ grabbed his hand with the balloon in it before he could throw it. Freeze turned around to look at JJ.

"Hey, pal. You want to join in on the fun?" Freeze asked JJ.

JJ just stood there staring at Freeze.

"OK, get your own balloon," Freeze told JJ, as he pointed to a blue milk crate full of water balloons.

Freeze reared back again to throw another balloon. This time JJ forcefully knocked the balloon out of his hand. A hush grew amongst the crowd.

Freeze faced JJ. He stood there startled for a minute. He looked into JJ's eyes and he read the fury in JJ's eyes. For a minute there, he stared silently at JJ. He then spoke.

"What the hell has gotten into you?" Freeze asked JJ.

JJ grabbed Freeze by the collar and pulled him so close to him, that their noses almost touched.

"That's enough!" JJ yelled at Freeze.

Freeze forcefully pulled himself away from JJ and he adjusted his collar.

"You trippin', man," Freeze replied to JJ.

"You taking up for this freak over your lifelong bud? Whatever happened to one for all and all-for-one. Ride together till we die. You going to take up for this retard over me. Your lifelong friend?" Freeze asked JJ.

"Oh yeah, one for all and all for one. Ride together till we die." JJ repeated this slogan back to Freeze.

"Let's see where that ended?" He asked Freeze standing there with his hand on his chin, like he was pondering over the question Freeze had asked him.

"Oh, yeah. Now I recall. That went out the door between you leaving me holding the rope at the flagpole and Mr. Jackson suspending me for two weeks. You left me hanging, bruh'." JJ told Freeze.

JJ went on to say to Freeze, "I mean, where have you been the past two weeks? No phone calls. Didn't come by the house. What's up?"

"Ok, that's how you feel. Suit yourself. You want to be the savior for this retard, go ahead. Our friendship is over!" Freeze told JJ as he stormed off of the scene.

"Fine with me. I don't need a backstabbing friend like you, anyway!" JJ yelled back at Freeze.

JJ looked at the funny-looking boy, standing there dripping wet and he turned back towards Freeze and yelled, "And as regards to his name. It's Benjamin!"

Freeze kept walking away, as he flipped JJ off with his middle finger.

JJ looked at the crowd and said to them, "You hear that. His name is Benjamin."

Some of the crowd began to whisper, "Benjamin."

JJ paused to look at the mob.

He then yelled to them, "That's right. His name is Benjamin."

JJ added, "And from now on, you got a problem with Benjamin, you got a problem with me."

A few people in the crowd again whispered the name, "Benjamin."

JJ looked around at the crowd once more.

He then yelled to them, "Man get out of here! It's nothing here to see!"

The crowd began to slowly disperse. JJ turned towards Benjamin, who was now standing there shivering and dripping wet.

"C'mon, Benjamin. Let's get you dry." JJ said to him.

He took Benjamin to the men's bathroom. JJ led Benjamin to one of the toilet stalls.

"Go in there and take all your clothes off and hand them over the door to me." He told Benjamin.

"OK," Benjamin said to JJ, in his childlike voice.

Benjamin did as he was instructed to do by JJ. JJ stood at the hand dryer for about fifteen minutes drying Benjamin's clothes. He then handed the clothes back over the stall to Benjamin.

"Get dressed and come out," JJ told Benjamin.

Benjamin got dressed and opened the stall door. He had his shoes on the wrong feet.

"Man, zip up your pants and button up your shirt, right? I mean, who wears button-ups nowadays anyway." JJ asked Benjamin.

JJ continued to critique Benjamin's attire.

"Straighten up your collar and put your shoes on the right feet. Here sit down. Let me help you." JJ told Benjamin.

As Benjamin sat on the commode, JJ chuckled to himself. He reminded himself of his mother when she was fussing at him.

"Runs in the family." He said under his breath.

JJ finished helping Benjamin get dressed.

"There, looking sharp as a tack, bruh'," JJ said to him, as he put his fist out to give Benjamin a fist bump.

In response to JJ trying to give him a fist bump, Benjamin covered up his face with his arms, as if he was going to be hit.

"No, Benji, baby boi'." JJ said to him as he pulled Benjamin out of the stoop position he had gone into.

"Fist bump." He told Benjamin, as he took his fist and bumped it together with Benjamin's fist.

Benjamin smiled at JJ and said to him, "We are friends,"

JJ became enraged at what Benjamin had just said to him.

He grabbed Benjamin by the collar and he told him, "Don't ever do that. We are not friends. You understand!"

"Ok." A subdued Benjamin said to JJ, with a quiver in his timid voice.

JJ relaxed and put his arm around Benjamin and he told him, "I'm sorry, Benjamin. I just got a reputation to uphold. You understand, don't you?"

"Ok," Benjamin replied to JJ.

"C'mon playa'. Let's get to class." JJ told Benjamin.

JJ walked Benjamin to his class. He then went to his own class.

CHAPTER 6 BENJI GETS A NEW NAME

The next day JJ was running to his music class. He reached the entrance just before the bell rang.

Miss Taylor, a thin older Black lady, was standing at the door of his music class. She was slim and pretty for her age. Only the gray hairs around the crown of her perm told off her age.

"Hold it, young man. You need to go to the office." She told him, as she stopped him at the door.

"But, Miss Taylor, I made it before the bell rang." JJ pled with her.

"I know you did, sweetie, but Mr. Johnson wants to see you in his office." She told him.

"Oh yes, ma'am." He said to her as he left her classroom to go to the principal's office.

"What now?" JJ thought to himself, as he walked to the office.

"Looks like I'm going to spend the whole school year in the principal's office." He mumbled to himself.

JJ was greeted by Miss Summers at the office door.

She told him, "Mr. Johnson is waiting on you in his office."

JJ stepped into Mr. Johnson's office. He was greeted by Mr. Johnson and Coach Smith.

Coach Smith was the basketball coach. He was a short, muscular, Black guy, who stood about 5'6", with a clean-shaven head and a full mustache and beard. He had a short man's complex. He was like a miniature TV series, Mr. T.

"Come on in, Mr. Jenkins. You know Coach Smith, don't you?" Mr. Johnson asked JJ.

"Yes, sir," JJ responded to him, as he put his right hand out to shake the coach's hand.

The coach just stared at JJ sternly with his arms folded. He refused to acknowledge JJ's hand. JJ slowly withdrew his hand from Coach Smith and he had a seat.

"Oh, boy. What did I do now?" JJ wondered.

"Let's get to the point, son. The other day there was an incident with this Swisher kid." Mr. Johnson started to say to JJ.

JJ interrupted Mr. Johnson's conversation and he jumped up out of his seat and said to them, "But sir, I tried to help him out!"

"I know you did, son. Please, don't interrupt me." Mr. Johnson said to JJ, as sternly as he could in his soft-spoken voice.

"Sorry, sir," JJ said to him as he sat back down in his seat.

"What I was saying, Mr. Jenkins, before you interrupted me is, I have talked to Coach Smith. He tells me you are an intricate part of both the basketball team and the football team." Mr. Johnson told JJ

Both Mr. Johnson and JJ looked toward Coach Smith. The coach nodded at them once, with an expressionless look on his face.

Mr. Johnson added, "So, therefore, I am going to uplift your 2-games suspension for football."

A big smile came on JJ's face, but it instantly disappeared when he saw the cold expression of discontent on Coach Smith's face.

"Thank you, sir." JJ hesitantly said to Mr. Johnson.

"One catch though, son." Mr. Johnson added.

"Uh oh, here we go. Detention after school or trash pickup." JJ thought to himself as the possible consequences he could be made to do rolled through his mind.

"Mr. Jenkins, have you thought of what you are going to do for your Senior Project?" Mr. Johnson asked JJ.

"Senior Project, I am a jock. Something in sports probably." JJ said to Mr. Johnson.

He then said, "I mean it's not due till May 3. I have plenty of time to think of something, sir."

"Well, Mr. Jenkins, don't work on it anymore. I have talked to Miss Taylor, your homeroom teacher, and Mr. Smith and I have come up with the perfect senior class project for you." Mr. Johnson told JJ.

"You have?" JJ inquired of Mr. Johnson, as he looked at Coach Smith.

For the first time, Coach Smith smiled. Not that happy smile, but a devious smile. He gave JJ the thumbs-up "ok" sign and he winked his right eye at him.

"Yes, son. Mr. Jenkins, we have decided that you will be a perfect mentor for Mr. Swisher for the remainder of the school year." Mr. Johnson told JJ.

A shocked look came upon JJ's face. He looked at Mr. Smith. Mr. Smith just smiled at him, nodding his head in affirmation.

JJ took a big gulp and he said to them, "But sir, I have never been a mentor before."

"Well, Mr. Jenkins, it's about time you learned. Don't you think so Mr. Smith?" Mr. Johnson asked Mr. Smith.

Mr. Smith remained silent. He just nodded his head in agreement.

"Yes, sir." A disappointed JJ said to Mr. Johnson as he sank down in his seat.

Sensing the uneasiness in JJ, Mr. Johnson said to him, "I tell you what, son. I am going to take your suspension off of your record."

He took some papers out of his desk and he ripped them up.

"How is that? Like it never happened." He told JJ.

"Thank you, sir," JJ replied dryly.

"Well, that will be all. You may be dismissed. Thank you, Mr. Jenkins. Thank you, Mr. Smith." Mr. Johnson said to the both of them.

They (JJ and Mr. Smith) both exited Mr. Johnson's office together. JJ turned to Mr. Smith and he put his hand out to shake Mr. Smith's hand.

"Thank you again, sir," JJ told Mr. Smith.

Mr. Smith looked at JJ's hand.

He then firmly grabbed his hand and said to him, "No, boy. Thank you. Because of you, I got a retardo' in my locker room as a towel boy." He told JJ with a snarl in his voice.

JJ began to grimace in pain from the tight hold Mr. Smith had on his hand.

Mr. Smith then said to JJ, "Now you listen to me, boy. It is your responsibility to keep that retardo' kid out of my hair. You understand?"

"Mr. Smith, this is my shooting hand you are squeezing, sir," JJ said to him, as he winced in pain and he appealed to Mr. Smith to release his hand.

Mr. Smith eased up on his grip on JJ's hand and he slowly turned away and walked away from JJ.

As he walked away he reminded JJ, "Retardo' kid is your responsibility."

JJ shook the sting of Mr. Smiths handshake off of his hand and he went to his class.

As he arrived at class and entered the classroom, he observed sitting in the front of the classroom, was Benjamin. JJ put a book to the side of his face and he tried to slip to the back of the class. He was stopped by Miss Taylor.

"Mr. Jenkins." He heard Miss Taylor call his name.

"Yes, ma'am," JJ answered her.

He dropped the book down from out over his face.

"We have reserved a special seat up front for you. My instructions are that you are to sit with Mr. Swisher." She told him.

The whole class erupted into laughter. JJ got up in disgust and he slowly went to the front of the class to sit next to Benjamin. Benjamin looked over at JJ and waved at him.

"Humiliating." JJ thought to himself.

It seemed like time went so slow in that class. JJ thought this class was the longest class he had ever been in. Finally, the bell rang.

"Thank, God," JJ said under his breath.

He was glad to get away from Benjamin. Only to find out that in the next class and each of his classes that day, Benjamin was there to greet him. The teacher in each of his classes had instructions that JJ was to sit next to Benjamin.

"Embarrassing." JJ thought to himself.

The last class was gym class. Freeze was in the class with JJ this period. JJ walked up to Freeze to talk to him. Freeze turned away from JJ and talked to a mutual friend of theirs, Big Mo.

"Can you tell him that I'm not speaking to him?" Freeze asked Big Mo to do it.

JJ turned around and told Freeze, as he walked away from him, "That's fine with me."

Freeze told Big Mo, "Tell JJ, maybe his new friend could be his basketball portna'."

JJ said to Freeze, "We don't need other people to talk for us. We can stop talking to each other, altogether."

Freeze said to Big Mo, "Tell him I don't need him as a portna'. He could be replaced by anybody."

JJ responded to him and told him, "Oh, yeah."

Freeze said to JJ, "Yeah."

Big Mo told the two of them, "Look, y'all two are trippin' if you think I am going to be the go-between for the two of you."

The two of them, (JJ and Freeze), stood there in each other's faces arguing with each other over frivolous matters. In the meantime, Benjamin and Big Mo were shooting the basketball around on the court.

Benjamin walked out onto the court while Big Mo was shooting the basketball. Big Mo began to pass the ball to Benjamin. Benjamin took a shot from the free-throw line. He made it.

Benjamin took another pass from Big Mo. Benjamin took a shot from the top of the key and he made it.

Big Mo passed the ball back to Benjamin, again. Big Mo tried to get JJ's and Freeze's attention so they could watch Benjamin shoot the ball.

"Look, guys." Big Mo called out to them.

JJ and Freeze continued to argue with each other. Big Mo tried to get their attention again.

"Look, guys!" Big Mo called out to JJ and Freeze, again.

They continued to argue. Big Mo took his shoe off and threw it at them.

He yelled at them and he said to them, "Look over here!"

He finally got the two to stop arguing with each other for enough time to get their attention. Big Mo threw the ball to Benjamin. Benjamin shot the ball from the right corner and he made it.

Big Mo passed the ball to Benjamin again. Benjamin shot the ball from the right corner again and he made it.

Big Mo passed the ball back to Benjamin. Benjamin made the basket from the left corner.

Big Mo passed the ball back to Benjamin. Benjamin made it from the half-court line.

"Well, look at that. The little munchkin can shoot the ball." Freeze said to them, as he rubbed Benjamin's head.

"Leave him alone. Why are you always bullying people? He's not messing with anybody." JJ told Freeze.

Freeze said to JJ, "Well, ok, mother duck. Let me leave you alone with your little duckling."

Freeze then stormed off of the court out of the gym. JJ asked Big Mo for the ball. He began passing the ball to Benjamin. Benjamin made 12 shots in a row. Each time JJ passed him the ball, Benjamin made the shot.

"Wow, who would have thought?" JJ asked Big Mo.

JJ then said to Big Mo, "Hey, Big Mo, this is our secret weapon. Wait till we tell Coach. Matter of fact, I've got a new name for him, instead of Benjamin."

"Oh, yeah. What's his new name?" Big Mo inquired of JJ.

JJ informed Big Mo, "From now on, Benjamin, you will be known as Swish. Do you like that name, Benjamin?" JJ asked Benjamin.

Benjamin nodded his head up and down with a big grin on his face.

"Ok, Swish it is," JJ told Benjamin.

Big Mo came over to JJ and he said to him, "OK, if you're gonna' do this. We gotta do it right."

JJ told Big Mo, "OK, come over here, Swish."

JJ walked over to the bleachers and he stood up on one of the bleachers. Benjamin walked over to JJ next to the bleachers. JJ stood over Swish. Big Mo came and stood next to them with his hand in a position to give a salute. JJ began his incantation.

"All right, hear ye, hear ye. We officially dub thee, once known as Benjamin A. Swisher, to be hereby known as Swish."

Big Mo saluted and made the sound of a trumpet as JJ finished his incantation.

Big Mo then asked JJ, "What's the "A" stand for?"

JJ answered him by saying to him, "I don't know. I don't know if he even has a middle name. I just added that in there because it sounded more official." JJ explained to Big Mo.

"Oh, I guess his name with a middle initial does sound more official." Big Mo told JJ.

The bell rang and the three boys ran out of the gym.

CHAPTER 7 THE FIELD TRIP

The next day was the first big field trip of the year. It was time for his class to go to the concert to listen to some boring music, but they didn't mind. They would do anything to get out of class.

The big blue bus came, and the kids rushed to get on the bus. Freeze and JJ got on the bus, but unlike other times they sat separately. Swish got on the bus, but no one would let him sit next to them.

Finally, the music teacher, Miss Taylor, got on the bus. She looked around the bus and led Swish to sit next to JJ. The kids began to laugh.

"Man, on the bus, too? Can't I get a break sometime?" JJ complained to her.

"He is your responsibility." Miss Taylor told JJ.

Everybody laughed at JJ, but nobody laughed harder than Freeze.

"Yeah, babysitter," Freeze said to him, as he teased JJ.

JJ just rolled his eyes at Freeze as he sat down disgustedly in his seat.

"Hi, JJ," Swish said waving his hand to JJ.

"Look, don't say anything to me," JJ warned Swish not to do it.

"Ok," Swish responded to him sadly, as he sank back down into his seat.

The bus arrived at the amphitheater at about 10 am. The music was playing already. Everyone got off of the bus and Miss Taylor got them all in two lines.

"Ok, boys this way and girls that way." She told them.

"JJ, hold Mr. Swisher's hand." Miss Taylor told JJ to do it.

The kids began to laugh. Patricia Torres began to make funny baby noises.

"Don't let the baby get away." She said to JJ, as she made baby faces to coincide with the noises she was making.

"Oh, that's so sweet," Freeze commented to JJ as he taunted JJ.

Reluctantly, JJ held Swish's hand, as they went into the auditorium. Everyone entered the auditorium and took a seat as the music was already playing. Sure enough, as the slow music played, JJ got sleepy and he dozed off to sleep.

As he slept, he could hear the serene music playing in the background. He was awakened by the voice of Miss Taylor calling his name.

"Wake up, JJ. It's time to go." She whispered into his ear.

As Miss Taylor got the group together and the boys and girls began to line up, they were still listening to the piano being played in the background. As they got ready to depart the amphitheater, Miss Taylor got a count of the kids. She kept coming up one short.

"Who is missing?" She asked the group.

Everybody looked around.

Finally, someone asked them, "Where is Benjamin?"

"Where is Mr. Jenkins?" Miss Taylor asked the group.

Everybody looked at JJ and they asked him, "Where is Benjamin?"

JJ looked puzzled and he put his arms up in the air as if to say, "I don't know."

"Ooh, you in trouble, now. You done let retardo' monster lose in the city." Freeze told JJ, with his hand in JJ's face.

JJ swiped at Freeze's hand, but Freeze moved his hand in time that JJ missed him. Everyone started looking for Swish now. The music playing in the background appeared to have gotten louder.

JJ was frantically looking all over for Swish. He walked up to one of the girls in the class who was standing at the entrance of the auditorium. She was looking at what was going on atop the stage. She had a starry glaze in her eyes. JJ saw it was Maria. He walked up to her. She was so transfixed on what was happening on the stage that she didn't notice him walk up to her.

"Maria," JJ said to her, as he called her name.

She said nothing to him. She just kept staring ahead. She was transfixed, staring at the stage.

"Maria." He called her name again.

She still said nothing to him. He called her again. This time he snapped his fingers in front of her face. She jumped as if she was coming out of a trance.

"Oh hi, JJ." She said to him.

"Maria, we're looking for Swish. Have you seen him?" JJ asked her.

She slowly shook her head up and down to indicate, "Yes, she had seen him."

"You have. Where is he?" JJ asked her.

She looked at JJ with a bewildered stare. She then slowly pointed up to the stage.

JJ looked up at the stage. He squinted through the bright stage lights to see who was on stage. On stage was Swish. He was playing classical music on the piano. Now JJ was transfixed, looking at Swish on the stage playing the piano.

One by one, everyone in the class came to see what Maria and JJ were looking at. Each person, including Miss Taylor, was speechless when they saw Swish up there playing classical music on the piano. The last person to come and watch was Freeze.

"Well, did we find retardo'?" Freeze jokingly asked them.

"Shush." Everybody told Freeze.

Freeze saw that everyone was looking forward to the stage. He looked towards the stage and he stepped forward to get a better look. Freeze saw Swish on the piano. He was playing Tchaikovsky, then Mozart, then Beethoven, then Bach, then Shubert.

Freeze was speechless. All of a sudden, everyone stopped what they were doing and started looking at Swish playing classical music on the piano. They were all looking in amazement at this young man playing on the piano.

Everyone who was looking was awestruck and amazed. Who would've thought that such an odd boy would be playing the piano?

Even the members of the orchestra had stopped to watch Swish play on the piano. Nobody moved. Even Miss Taylor stood there in amazement. Everyone in the auditorium just stood there, star-struck. Not knowing what to say.

Finally, Swish played the last note. He closed the piano, got up, went to center stage, took a bow, and walked down off of the stage. Everyone just stared at him as they made a path for him to walk through the gathering that had stopped to watch him.

The group of students followed him to the bus. No one said a word. Swish just walked to the bus and he got on the bus. He went to the back of the bus and he laid down on the back seat. He curled up and he went to sleep.

Everybody got on the bus without saying a word. All eyes were on Swish. The silence was deafening. Everyone sat on the bus quietly. Even Miss Taylor sat without saying a word.

Even Freeze, the class clown. Even he was quiet and not joking around as he usually was. When Freeze got on the bus, he saw Swish lying down on the back of the bus. Freeze started to go towards the back of the bus where Swish was lying down.

Thinking he was going to do something detrimental to Swish, JJ got up to stop him. Big Mo stopped JJ and pushed JJ back down into his seat.

"Relax, it's cool. Just watch." Big Mo told JJ.

Freeze walked back to the seat Swish was lying on and he took his jacket off and covered Swish up with it. Freeze then walked back to his seat.

He looked back at Swish and said to the group, "He is special."

Freeze looked back at Swish one more time and he said again to the group, "Yeah, he is special. We have to take care of him."

He then took his seat on the bus.

On the entire trip back on the bus, there was silence. When the bus got back to the school, Miss Taylor asked JJ to speak to him.

"Yes, Miss Taylor," JJ answered her.

Miss Taylor reminded JJ that she had assigned Swish to him and that his failure in this assignment would reflect upon his semester grade.

"I understand, Miss Taylor," JJ told her, as he left the room.

When JJ got back home, his mother asked him how his field trip went.

He told her, "Okay, I guess."

He went on to tell her about what had happened with Swish.

"Wow, that's amazing." She told him.

There was a moment of silence.

He then told her, "Ma, I am burnt out."

She asked him, "Why, baby?"

He told her, "Ma, it is a hard task keeping up with Swish."

She advised him, "Well, pray about it, baby."

There was another moment of silence.

JJ then said to her, "Mom, every time I mention a problem. You say pray about it, but why would God curse me to put me in this situation?" He asked his mother.

"Well, baby. You saw what Swish did today?" She asked him.

"Yeah, Ma, I did." He answered her.

She then asked him, "Would you say Swish is special?"

JJ thought about her question.

He then answered her and he said to her, "Yes, ma'am. I would say he is special."

"Well son, you are asking God the wrong question." His mother told him.

"What do you mean, Ma?" He asked her.

His mother said to him, "If Swish is special and God has chosen you as his guardian. You should be asking God, what is so special about you that God saw fit to put you in charge of His special treasure like Swish? That out of all the people in the world, He put this responsibility on you."

She went on to say, "That's not a curse, son. That's an honor. God doesn't just choose anybody to do his work, son." She told him

JJ thought about what his mother had said to him.

He then asked her, "You mean God has appointed me as Swish's guardian angel?"

"Well, son. I wouldn't quite say an angel. You're not quite an angel yet, and I'm not in a rush for you to become one." She told him.

She went on to say to him, "But you are his appointed guardian down here on earth."

A moment of silence went by, as JJ thought about what his mother had just told him.

JJ then asked his mother, "Why me, Ma?"

His mother shook her head and she told him, "Wrong question again, son. The question is, why not you? You're thoughtful, you're smart, you're kind."

JJ chimed in, and he said to her, "I'm good-looking."

They both laughed at this comment that JJ had made. There was another moment of silence.

JJ then told his mother, "You know, Ma. I never looked at it that way. Thanks, Ma."

"You are welcome, son." She replied to him.

JJ looked at his mother and he asked her, "Why are you old people so smart?"

"Hey, the word is experienced, not old." She responded to him, as she corrected him.

They both laughed again. There was another moment of silence. JJ broke the silence again.

"Ma, I'm going to be the best guardian for God ever." He told her.

"I know you are, baby." His mother assured him.

He looked at his mother and he said to her, "Ma."

"Yes, son." She replied to him.

"Yo' lil Pookie love ya." He told her.

"Love you more, baby." His mother replied to him.

CHAPTER 8 THE LOWER BOTTOMS

After the school field trip, JJ felt an obligation to kind of watch over Swish. He started spending more and more time with Swish.

On this day, JJ and Swish were out in the park playing on the basketball courts.

Freeze came down to the basketball courts. He saw Swish and JJ playing basketball. He watched them for about five minutes, as they were shooting the ball.

JJ started feeding Swish the ball. Swish was shooting the ball from all over the court. He was making most of his shots.

Freeze came over to stand next to JJ. JJ rolled his eyes at Freeze and he turned away from him. The two haven't spoken since they blew up against each other before the field trip.

They stood next to each other watching Swish shoot the ball from all over the court, mostly making it.

Finally, Freeze said to JJ, "Lil retar'"— he caught himself from saying the word retard and he rephrased what he was about to say.

He then corrected himself and said to JJ, "I mean the lil' fella' can really shoot, can't he?"

JJ said nothing to Freeze. He just gave him a head nod. They both stood there in silence for a few minutes.

Freeze then said to JJ, "Okay this is killin' me."

He turned towards JJ and he said to him, "I'm sorry. I was wrong."

Freeze stooped to his knees with his hands clasped in prayer position and he said to JJ, "Please, please forgive me."

JJ turned towards Freeze.

He looked down at him on his knees and he told Freeze, "Get up from there. You look ridiculous."

JJ held his hand out to help Freeze up. He pulled Freeze to his feet and gave him a hug.

"It's all good," JJ said to Freeze.

Both of them stood there and they watched Swish shoot the ball.

Freeze said to JJ, "Man, that little guy really can shoot."

JJ replied to Freeze, "Yeah, he is a little Pistol Pete."

The two watch him for a few more minutes.

Freeze then asked JJ, "Where did he learn to shoot like that?"

JJ replied to him, "I don't know. Why don't you ask him?"

Freeze looked at Swish and addressed him.

"Hey, lil' man." Freeze started to say to him.

He then paused, looked at JJ, and asked him, "It's okay if I call him lil' man, right?"

JJ nodded his head.

Freeze called Swish again and said to him, "Lil' man."

Swish stopped shooting the ball and he looked at Freeze.

"Where did you learn to shoot like that?" Freeze asked Swish.

"Watching TV," Swish told him.

"Watching TV, huh?" Freeze said to him, repeating what Swish had said to him.

Freeze then asked JJ, "Where did he learn to play the piano like that?"

JJ said nothing. He just cut his eyes over towards Swish.

"Oh yeah," Freeze said to JJ.

Freeze turned his attention towards Swish and he asked him, "Hey bro, where did you learn to play the piano like that?"

Swish stopped dribbling the basketball and responded to Freeze and told him, "Watching TV."

"Watching TV. Imagine that." Freeze said in response to Swish's answer to him.

Freeze then said to JJ, "Geez, I ought to be a genius as much TV as I watch."

"Watching girls on TV doesn't count," JJ told Freeze.

The both of them laughed at this comment that JJ had made. As they stood there, Slim and Big Baby and a friend of theirs came and they played basketball on the other court.

Freeze looked over at Slim and he said to JJ, "Look at what the cat dragged in here?"

Slim only looked back at Freeze and he smiled at him.

"Relax now, please. We're not looking for any trouble today." JJ told Freeze.

Freeze got an idea. He whispered something into JJ's ear. He then went down to the other end of the court where Slim, Big Baby, and their friend were playing basketball.

"How's bout a little 3 on 3 fellas'?" He said to them, as he shook Big Baby's hand, but looked at Slim.

"I'm down. Put yo' money where yo' mouth is." Slim told Freeze.

Slim brought out $200 in $20 bills and he said to Freeze, "$200 says we win."

"You got it. Put up or shut up." Freeze told Slim.

Freeze walked over to JJ. JJ whispered into Freeze's ear.

"Man, we don't have no $200," JJ told Freeze.

"Relax man. I got this." Freeze told JJ.

Freeze then turned towards Slim and he said to him, "$200 it is."

Slim put ten $20 bills down on the ground.

He then looked around and he said to them, "One problem. Who's your third person?"

Freeze looked around as if he was looking for someone. He then looked over at Swish. At this time, Swish stood at the far end of the park away from them. Slim and his crew were unaware that Swish had come to the park with JJ and Freeze.

"We will take that guy over there," Freeze told Slim, as he pointed to Swish.

"Huh?" Slim said to Freeze, as he squinted across the park to look at Swish.

"Yeah, I choose that guy standing over there," Freeze said to Slim.

Slim looked over at Swish again and he said to Freeze, "You mean that weirdo-looking dude over there? Man, you feeling generous today. You might as well just give me $200."

Slim, Big Baby, and their friend faced off with Freeze, JJ, and Swish. They played a three-on-three basketball game.

"We will be Skins this time," Slim said to them.

Slim, Big Baby, and their friend took their shirts off and the game got started.

The game was no match. Freeze and JJ mostly passed the ball to Swish. Swish made it every time he shot the ball.

The final score was Freeze's team 24, Slim's team 12.

Freeze and JJ went to the middle of the court and they gave each other a high five to celebrate their victory.

Slim went down and he picked up the money that Freeze had laid on the court.

After he counted the money, he said to Freeze, "Hey, this ain't no $200. This is a couple of $20s and some ones."

Freeze walked over to Slim and he snatched the money out of Slim's hand. Slim and Freeze were now standing toe to toe with each other. They were readying to get into a physical confrontation.

Slim said to Freeze, "How do we know that you would've been good on our bet if we had won the game?"

Freeze said to Slim, "You don't want any of this, asshole."

The two positioned themselves into fight mode. They faced each other with their fists balled up. JJ and Big Baby ran down the court and got between them.

JJ said to Slim, as Big Baby held him back, "Slim, this is me, JJ. You know if you would have won, I'd been good for it."

Slim looked at JJ.

Slim then stepped back away from Freeze and said to him, "Man, you lucky I got mad love fo' yo' potna'."

Freeze went to pick up the rest of the money and he commented to Freeze, "It's $200 now."

Freeze was laughing as he counted the money in front of Slim's face.

"OK, you got me. All is fair in the game. No holds barred." Slim said to Freeze.

"Yeah, step off, asshole," Freeze told Slim as he handed Slim a $20 bill.

"Don't go away mad. Just go away." Freeze added.

Slim threw the $20 bill on the ground. He began to walk away. He then turned back around and he went back to get the $20 bill off of the ground.

"You owe me this," Slim told Freeze, as he picked the bill up off of the ground and walked away.

"See ya'. Wouldn't wanna be ya." Freeze added as he was counting the money and he was laughing about the scenario.

In the meantime, JJ was shaking hands with Big Baby and the other friend of Slim's.

"Nice game." They said, as they congratulated JJ and they walked off of the court.

Freeze stood there counting the money in front of them, as they walked off of the court, shaking their heads.

JJ walked over to Freeze and he said to him, "You need to chill out Freeze. Must you always gloat after we win?"

"Sorry, I can't help it. It's in my blood. My daddy was a playa'. Therefore, I am a playa'." Freeze told JJ.

"Yeah, I thought you said you never met your father," JJ said to Freeze.

"Nope, never met the man," Freeze told JJ.

"If you never met the man, how do you know he was a player?" JJ asked Freeze.

Freeze told JJ, "It's obvious. I got so much playa' in me. He had to be a playa'."

"Well, put this in your blood, "Playa' folks". Don't ever pull no shit like that again with me." He told Freeze.

"Ooh, I never heard you cuss," Freeze told JJ.

"Well hear me straight. The only asshole here today, was you. I don't play games like that. I play on the up and up." He told Freeze.

"Awright', sorry. My bad. Won't do it no mo'. Ok, but, I'm telling Miss Jenkins, that you were cussing." Freeze told JJ.

"That's fair enough, and I'm telling Emma Jones that you're dating Sarah Smith, too," JJ informed Freeze.

"Dang, JJ, you ain't' gotta' get all vicious wit' it and ere'thang'. Ok, truce." Freeze was offered to JJ.

"Yeah, that's what I thought," JJ said to Freeze.

They both did the pinky handshake and they came to an agreement.

JJ told Freeze, "Anyway, my mother would understand. Me dealing with you will make the Pope curse."

Freeze asked JJ, "How did you learn to blackmail people so well?"

JJ responded to him and he said to him, "Learned from the best, you."

"Dang, JJ, you make it seem like I'm scandalous or something," Freeze said to JJ.

JJ just looked at Freeze and he nodded his head to him. JJ then changed the subject.

"OK, anyway, enough small talk. Give me my money before you figure out a way to scam me for it, too." JJ told Freeze.

Freeze gave JJ $100.

JJ looked at the $100. He then looked at Swish and asked Freeze, "And what about Swish? He deserves something."

"Aw, man. We gotta' split it three ways? Lil man don't even know what to do with money." Freeze told JJ.

JJ just looked at Freeze with a stern look on his face. Freeze can't stand it when JJ looks at him that way and he caved in.

"OK, OK, man. Don't look at me like that. We will split it three ways." Freeze told JJ.

Freeze added, "But since we got $200. We might as well make some big money. Let's go to DeFremery Park and play the big boys for some real money." Freeze encouraged them to do.

"What, you mean to the lower bottoms? I don't know. That place is known as Dead Man's Park. Those homies are serious about their scrilla' over there. Besides, Ma doesn't want me over on that side of town. It's too much trouble to get into." JJ told Freeze.

Freeze said to JJ, "Stop being such a wus'. You gonna be a mama's boy all of your life? Baby boi', get some balls. Let's have some adventure for a change."

He added, "Live on the edge. Look at all the money we can make." Freeze told JJ.

JJ thought about what Freeze had said to him. He then decided to change it.

"OK, let's go for it. Come on, Swish." JJ said to Swish, as the three of them set out towards the other side of town. The rough side of town.

They arrived at DeFremery Park. On the basketball court, there were some big hairy men with tattoos on their bodies playing basketball. Rough-looking guys. Looked like the penitentiary courtyard. Freeze walked up to a guy in all black, who was wearing a white Stetson hat.

Whatcha' want, youngsta'?" The man asked Freeze, as Freeze walked up to him.

"I want to sign my team up," Freeze said to the man.

The man looked at Freeze up and down. The man was wearing dark sunglasses with a toothpick in his mouth.

He informed Freeze, "It's a hunned' dollas' a team per game. Winna' take half da' pot of those who are betting."

Freeze said nothing. He just nodded his head up and down to let the man know he agreed with those terms.

The man looked at Freeze and said to him, "Looka' yere', youngsta'. We real about our chedda' round' yere', ya' dig? So, no shenanigans."

Freeze gave the man a thumbs up.

The man went on to tell him, "Another thang', youngsta'. You and yo' potnas' look soft. Ain't' no choir boys round' yere'. There is a rough group that hangs out round' these parts. I ain't' responsible fo' yo' safety." He told Freeze, showing Freeze that he was packing heat by lifting his shirt up and showing him the piece that was strapped on his waistband.

Freeze just nodded his head once to the man and he gave the man $100.

Soon afterward, the games got started. They played the first game, and they won the first game.

"Look at there. See, now we got $300 to split. Like taking candy from a baby." Freeze told JJ.

JJ looked around at the crowd and he told Freeze, "More like taking a banana from a gorilla."

They played the next game and they won the next game. They played three more games and they won all three games.

They won each game they had played. They had $900 to split between the three of them. Now It was time for the last game.

"Winna' take one half of the pot of $5000!" The man in black announced to the crowd.

This would be $2500. If they won this pot. That added to the $900 they had already won would make it $1100 plus apiece they would have.

"See, if we win this. We get $3400 to split between us. That's some real scratch." Freeze told JJ.

Right now, there was a break in the action. Freeze went to the restroom. He stepped into one of the bathroom stalls and he closed the door. While he was in the stall, some other guys came into the bathroom. He heard the conversation of the two thugs.

"Who dat' is, dose' young punks who come in ere' winning e'erthang?" One of them said to the other one.

"Don't know?" The other guy that came into the bathroom said to his partner.

"Yeah, dey' betta' not win dis' last final game." The first guy said to the second guy.

"Yeah, whatcha' gonna' do ifn' they do." The second guy said to the first guy.

"I'm gonna' strip dem' suckas'." He told his friend.

"I feel ya'. I'm down wit' it. Give me a piece of dis' ere' action. I'm gonna hit dis' lick wit' ya'." The second guy said to the first guy.

Freeze was listening in on these guys' conversation. He started contemplating what he had gotten himself, Swish, and JJ into. He heard the two thugs slap their hands in a high five and they snapped their fingers before they exited the restroom. Freeze waited until he was sure the two guys had left out of the bathroom. He then rushed back to JJ and Swish.

"Looka' here. We gotta' problem." Freeze told JJ.

He told JJ of the plot he had heard of in the restroom.

"Man, I knew we should not have come over here," JJ complained to Freeze.

"Don't worry. I gotta' plan." Freeze assured JJ.

"Well, I hope this plan involves getting us outta' here in one piece," JJ said to Freeze.

"Relax, JJ. I got this." Freeze told JJ.

Freeze whispered into JJ's ear. The three of them then returned to the basketball courts.

The last game was about to get started. Just as in previous games, Freeze's team was winning the game. They only needed one shot to win.

Freeze stood outside of the court, ready to pass the ball in.

He passed the ball to Swish.

Swish shot the ball and he made it for the final score.

As soon as the ball went into the hoop, JJ ran, grabbed Swish by the hand, and took off running out of the park.

After they had run several blocks away from the park, JJ stopped to catch his breath. He waited for Freeze. He and Swish waited for more than two hours before, finally, Freeze ran up to them out of breath, with the money in his hands.

"Hey, what took you so long? I thought you had dangled' us." JJ told Freeze, while he was laughing.

Freeze handed the money over to JJ, and he then collapsed onto the ground. JJ noticed blood on the back of Freeze's shirt.

"Freeze!" JJ yelled to Freeze, as he watched him lying on the ground.

Freeze lay there on the ground bleeding.

"Get up, Freeze!" JJ yelled to him again.

This time JJ helped Freeze to his feet. There was a hospital across the street. JJ and Swish walked Freeze over to the hospital. JJ sat Freeze in a seat when they got into the clinic.

"We're gonna get you some help, potna'. Hang in there." JJ told Freeze.

JJ then walked up to a lady wearing a white uniform sitting at the counter.

"My friend, he needs help." Out of breath JJ told the lady.

The lady looked up at JJ and she asked him, "Does your friend have insurance?"

"Yes, no, I don't know. He needs help lady. He's hurt." A frantic JJ told the lady.

She gave JJ a stack of forms to fill out.

"Fill out these forms." She told JJ.

"Lady, he needs help now!" JJ screamed at her, as he threw the forms back at her.

One of the doctors overheard JJ. He walked over to him and he asked JJ, "Can I help you, young man?"

"Yes, sir. My friend, he's been injured. He needs help." JJ told the doctor, as he was almost hyperventilating.

The doctor stood there staring at JJ. JJ handed the doctor the money they had won in the park playing basketball.

"Here, we have $3400," JJ told the doctor, as he handed the doctor the winning pot.

The doctor handed the money back to JJ and he told him, "That won't be necessary. Put your money in your pocket."

The doctor then called for help.

"Nurse, get some interns over here and get this young man on a gurney." The doctor said to the nurse.

They put Freeze onto a gurney and they rolled him into the emergency room.

The next day JJ went back to the hospital. He went to the room where Freeze was housed in. Freeze was lying on his left side. A big smile came over his face when JJ walked into the room.

"Hey, man, you know there are easier ways of getting days off from school." JJ jokingly said to Freeze.

Freeze put a big grin on his face and he said to JJ, "I know dude, but those ways are too boring."

JJ sat on the side of Freeze's bed and they both laughed at Freeze's joke. They sat quietly for a minute.

JJ then asked Freeze, "Why did you do that?"

Freeze asked JJ "Why did I do what?"

"Why did you risk yourself for Swish and me?" JJ asked Freeze.

"I mean, I don't know. I guess I felt responsible for you two. I didn't want anything to happen to Swish and I definitely didn't want to have to go back to your mother to have to tell her that you got injured because of me. I'd rather face World War Three. Anyway, it was just a flesh wound." Freeze told JJ.

"A flesh wound? Eight stitches. You could run a flatbed truck through it. Doc said it was 2 inches away from your kidney." JJ informed Freeze

JJ went on to tell Freeze, "Well anyway, next time this happens. We are all in this together." JJ assured Freeze.

"Exactly." A voice came from outside of the door.

"We are all in this together." The voice said to them.

Freeze and JJ looked up at the door. In the door walked in Slim and Big Baby and two other guys.

"Wssup' fellas'?" Freeze said to them.

Big Baby and Slim walked over and they shook Freeze's hand and gave him a little hug.

"Yeah, you guys are foolish going on the other side of town by yourselves. Next time you decide to do a fool thang' like that. Holla' at yo' boi'." Slim told them.

"Word up," Freeze told Slim.

After a short visit, Slim and his buddies began to exit the room.

"You guys stay up," Slim told them, as he and his crew left the room.

"We gotta' go down the hallway and see Big Baby's Grammy." He informed them.

They say goodbye to Slim and his crew.

As Slim's crew left the room, Freeze told JJ, "Wow, I didn't know Slim cared."

"Yeah, Slim is cool people," JJ told Freeze.

They both then said in unison, "For an asshole."

They both laughed at this joke they had just made.

JJ then asked Freeze, "Hey, how long are you gonna' be in this hospital?"

Freeze told JJ, "Doctor said I should be outta' here by tomorrow."

"OK, you know we still gotta' get ready for football season," JJ told Freeze.

Freeze gave JJ a thumbs up and he said to him, "Oh, I'm ready. Bring it on."

JJ and Freeze embraced each other and JJ left to go home.

CHAPTER 9 FOOTBALL SEASON

It was the third week of September. It was time for the football season to start. JJ and Freeze were on the practice field. As usual, Swish was there as their sidekick.

Coach Ferrero, the football coach, was easier going than Coach Smith, the basketball coach. He even got Swish a uniform for the team and he put Swish on the team as an extra.

JJ was kind of getting used to Swish hanging around him. Matter of fact, the whole team was fond of Swish. He was like the team mascot.

Because of JJ, his superstar quarterback, the coach put Swish on the roster. Unlike basketball, the school had never been competitive in baseball and football.

In the three years JJ and Freeze had been on the team, the school had won only four games out of 30. So, there was no big expectation for the football season.

The first game they played was against Hogan High. Hogan High was probably the only team worse than they were. As expected, they beat Hogan High, 12 to nothing in a low-scoring game.

The next team they played was Lakeside High. Lakeside was one of the teams predicted to compete in the playoffs. In the best game, JJ and Freeze had played in their high school careers. They pulled off an upset of Lakeside High. They won a close game. The score was 35 to 32.

The next game was even closer. It was against a more potent opponent, The Dogwood Dragons. They were 12-point underdogs to Dogwood, but they ended up winning the game by a score of 21 to 20.

For the first time in the four years that JJ and Freeze had been at AT Hligh, the team had a chance to get into the playoffs.

The next game was against Bush High. Again, they were underdogs to Bush High, but AT High ended up winning a squeaker. The score was AT High 27 to Bush High's 25.

Next on the schedule was Danville. If they beat Danville, they would go to the divisional championship game against Scottsdale.

The game against Danville was a ferocious game. The score went back and forth, but in the end, AT High won on a last-second field goal.

For the first time, JJ and Freeze had led their team to the divisional championship game. The next opponent they played was powerful Scottsdale.

In the three previous years that JJ and Freeze were at AT High School, Scottsdale had won three state titles and only lost one game. That was to Douglas Dogwood. The last time AT High played Scottsdale High, they lost to them by a score of 35 to 0.

Now it's time for the playoffs. Scottsdale, being undefeated again, stormed into the playoffs easily. They were beating their opponents by an average of 30 points a game.

AT High was to play Scottsdale for the regional championship. It was a week before the championship game. The team was at practice on the AT High football field.

The players were throwing the ball around. JJ threw a pass to Freeze. The pass went over Freeze's head. Swish ran to get the ball. He then started running downfield with the ball. He kept running even, after the other players tried to stop him.

All the players chased Swish to try and get the ball from him. Swish dodged all of them. He was able to dodge everyone trying to stop him till he made it to the end zone. When he got into the end zone, he did a little victory dance. JJ finally caught up with him.

"Swish, stop playing and give us the ball!" A frustrated JJ yelled at him, as he snatched the ball away from Swish.

"Sorry," Swish said to JJ, in his childish voice.

Remembering how sensitive Swish was, JJ put his arm around him and said to him, "It's ok, Swish."

In the meantime, Freeze was just nodding his head looking at Swish. He was trying to figure out how they could use Swish in a game.

A week later, the team was pumped up about the game they were going to have against Scottsdale for the regional championship.

The game started off disappointingly, though. Scottsdale scored touchdowns on its first two possessions. At the end of the first quarter, the score was 14 to nothing in favor of Scottsdale. It looked like Scottsdale was going to rout AT High again.

The Scottsdale High School players were already giving each other high fives as if they had already won the game.

At the end of the first quarter, the AT coach decided to put his best players playing on defense and offense. Two of those players were JJ and Freeze.

At halftime, the score was 14 to nothing in favor of Scottsdale. The coach of AT High had stopped the bleeding, in that he had stopped Scottsdale from scoring again, but AT High could not score on Scottsdale's superior defense.

At halftime, the coach gave the team a pep talk. The coach figured out that if they could keep Scottsdale from scoring, they had a chance of winning the game.

Halftime ended and the two teams were back on the field for the third quarter. The third quarter was scoreless. Now it was time for the fourth quarter.

The fourth quarter began with Scottsdale waiting to receive the kickoff from AT High. The ball was kicked off to Scottsdale. They received it on their 30-yard line. The Scottsdale runner caught the ball and began running with it.

Just as the runner was going to be tackled, he pitched the ball back to another Scottsdale runner and this runner ran the ball over 50 yards for a touchdown. The Scottsdale kicker kicked the extra point.

Now the score was 21 to nothing, in favor of Scottsdale. The score seemed to be insurmountable.

As time ticked down off of the clock, the Scottsdale fans and team began to celebrate prematurely. They could feel victory in the air.

With five minutes to go, Scottsdale had to kick off the ball to AT High. Freeze was observing the field. He whispered something into the coach's ear.

The coach called for a time-out. Freeze had an idea. He whispered the idea into the coach's ear. The coach was desperate, so he was willing to try anything.

The coach looked at Freeze and he said to him, "This had better work."

Freeze told the coach, "Trust me, coach. I got this. When the play works, you can take the credit for it."

Scottsdale went to kick off the ball. This time AT High lined up on the field with Swish in the backfield. The ball was kicked off to AT High. Freeze receives the punt. He ran a couple of steps with the ball and he lateraled the ball back to JJ.

JJ ran a couple of steps with the ball and he lateraled the ball back to Swish. Swish just stood there holding the ball.

JJ yelled to Swish, "Run, Swish!"

Upon hearing JJ telling him to run, Swish began to run with the ball downfield. Scottsdale teammates began to chase after him. The speedy and evasive Swish ran the length of the field to the end zone.

"Touchdown!" The man in stripes yelled out, as he raised his hands, as Swish crossed over the goal line.

Finally, AT High was on the scoreboard. AT High made its extra point and now the score was Scottsdale 21, AT High 7.

"Now we're cooking with grease. Defense, let's hold 'em." The coach of AT High said to his team.

Once again, the AT High defense held the Scottsdale team from scoring. Now three minutes were remaining in the game. Once again Swish was on the field to receive the ball.

Last time they caught Scottsdale off guard using Swish. This time, the Scottsdale players would be ready for the speedy, evasive Swish, or so they thought.

Once again, the ball was kicked off to AT High. This time the ball went straight to Swish. JJ and Freeze were right in front of him to block for him this time.

Swish ran downfield with JJ and Freeze blocking for him. They blocked the first two Scottsdale players who tried to tackle Swish. Swish got away from another player and evaded a tackle from a fourth player. Again, Swish outran the rest of the field. Again, the referee raised his arms.

"Touchdown!" The official yelled out to the crowd.

Now the AT High crowd was ecstatic and the Scottsdale crowd, for the first time in four years, was nervous. Swish antics had snatched the smell of victory out of the air for Scottsdale.

Now, after the kicker of AT High made the extra point, the score was Scottsdale 21 to AT High's 14.

The problem now was there was only a minute left in the game and AT High was down by seven points. To complicate the situation more, they were kicking off the ball to Scottsdale.

Their only hope was to kick an onside kick. The coach for AT High lined the team up to do an onside kick. Both teams' lineups were ready to fight for the ball.

The AT High kicker squib kicked the ball on the ground. A free-for-all all happened on the field for the football. There was a battle on the ground for the ball. Players from both teams were piled up on top of each other.

The referee went over to separate the teams. After the referee separated the two teams, JJ came out of the pile-up with the ball on AT High's 35-yard line. The AT High's side of the field erupted into cheers. While the Scottsdale side grumbled in dismay.

AT High's coach called for a timeout. They huddled up on the sidelines. The coach discussed a play with the team. They broke out of the huddle and they took their positions on the field.

Again, Swish was lined up on the far-right side of the field. The coach for Scottsdale High lined up three of his defensive players opposite Swish. JJ took his position behind the center. The ball was hiked to him.

JJ stepped back like he was going to throw the ball to Swish. Practically the whole Scottsdale defense gravitated towards Swish.

JJ paused and he pulled the ball back. He looked towards the end zone. Freeze was standing in the end zone by himself. JJ floated the ball to Freeze who was standing in the end zone. Freeze caught the ball with ease.

"Touchdown!" The referee yelled out to the crowd with his hands up in the air.

Freeze went into his touchdown dance. The AT High crowd went wild, while the Scottsdale crowd gave out a sigh of disgust. Now the score was Scottsdale 21 to AT High's 20.

AT High's coach called for a timeout. A discussion was held on the sidelines with the team. Again, AT High came out of the huddle with Swish in the lineup. AT High had decided to go for the two-point conversion for the win, instead of the extra point for the tie. The Scottsdale team seemed more confused than ever now.

When the next play started, half of the Scottsdale team went towards Freeze, who was lined up on the left opposite end, and the other half went towards Swish, who was lined up on the right end.

AT High got into formation with JJ behind the center. The ball was hiked by the center to JJ.

This time JJ faked throwing the ball to Freeze. He then lateraled the ball to Swish. Swish just stood there holding the ball.

"Run, Swish!" JJ yelled out for Swish to do.

Swish started running with the ball, but he ran in the wrong direction. He had 21 other players from Scottsdale and AT High chasing after him.

Freeze was the only one who could outrun him and he caught him before he crossed the wrong goal line.

"The other way, Swish! The other way!" Freeze yelled for Swish to run the other way.

Swish turned about and he started running down the field in the opposite direction. Freeze picked off the first defensive player trying to tackle him.

Another Scottsdale player came at Swish and Swish ran 10 yards backwards to evade this player.

Two other Scottsdale players came at Swish, as he reached the 32-yard line of AT High. Swish ran sideline to sideline to evade them.

Now Swish was at the 50-yard line.

Swish picked up a block from JJ and he picked up another block from another AT High player. He had managed to make it to the 30-yard line of Scottsdale.

One more player stood in the way between Swish and the goal line. The player lunged at Swish. Swish ducked and the Scottsdale player flew over his head.

Now Swish ran everybody behind him and he crossed the goal line as time ran out.

The exhausted referee raised both of his arms and in a hoarse voice he yelled out to the crowd, "Score!"

The sound of the starter pistol rang out. It signaled the end of the game.

"Two-point conversion." The referee said to the crowd in his hoarse voice.

The Scottsdale fans became eerily silent, whereas the AT High fans erupted into cheers and they rushed onto the field. The field was strewn with players from both sides of the field. They collapsed from exhaustion while they had tried to chase Swish down.

Both Freeze and JJ lifted up Swish on their shoulders and all of the AT High fans were chanting, "S-W-I-S-H," "S-W-I-S-H," "S-W-I-S-H," "S-W-I-S-H," as they carried Swish off of the field with the scoreboard showing Scottsdale 21 and AT High 22.

Freeze asked Swish, sitting up on his and JJ's shoulders, "Where did you learn how to run a football like that, buddy?"

"Watching TV," Swish responded to him.

"Watching TV," Freeze said, as he repeated what Swish had said to him.

"Figures," JJ said to them.

"We are going to go get some Rock n' Roll (Rocky Road) ice cream," JJ told Swish.

"Yay," Swish yelled out, as they left the stadium with Swish still hoisted on JJ's and Freeze's shoulders. They were on their way to the ice cream parlor.

CHAPTER 10 BASKETBALL AND BASEBALL SEASON

September and October went by really fast. So now it was time for a high school basketball game in November.

JJ was the starting shooting guard for the team along with Freeze as the starting point guard and Big Mo was the starting center on the team. The Robinson twins played starting forwards. Guerrero and White were part of the bench. Since Swish was to follow JJ around, they made him the team mascot and the water/towel boy.

Being with the team helped improve Swish's image. Not only had JJ and Freeze appointed themselves as Swish's personal guardians, but people loved Swish's childlike carefree personality. That was everybody, but Coach Smith.

Coach Smith still resented having to have Swish with the team. He often verbally abused Swish.

Coach Smith called Swish names like psycho, dumbo', stupid, idiot, but his favorite name for Swish was retardo'.

One day Freeze told JJ, "Coach Smith sure is hard on Swish, isn't he?"

JJ looked over at Coach Smith going into one of his tirades against Swish and he responded to Freeze and he said to him, "Yeah man, but we can't say anything and risk ourselves of being thrown off of the team."

JJ looked back at the coach going off on his tirade against Swish. He was berating Swish for any little thing he did.

JJ added, "I guess."

"Yeah, I guess you're right," Freeze told JJ.

The chastisement didn't seem to bother Swish at all. He was the team gofer and he seemed to enjoy it.

On one such occasion, in the middle of practice, while the coach was giving the boys a pep talk. Swish came to Coach Smith with a towel. Coach Smith turned red in the face and he went on one of his tirades.

"No, you bungling idiot! I said my clipboard! Not a towel!" He yelled at Swish, as he knocked the towel out of Swish's hand.

"You damn fool! Get out of here!" Coach Smith yelled for Swish to do.

Tears began to well up in Swish's eyes.

"Sorry," Swish said to him, in his timid childlike voice.

"Sorry, hell! Get the hell out of here!" Coach Smith yelled at him, as he grabbed Swish by the arm and he pulled him to the exit.

"Sorry." A tearful Swish said to him again.

"Yeah, you're sorry all right! I want your sorry ass out of my gym!" Coach Smith yelled out for Swish to do.

"Get the hell out of here!" He told Swish, as he pushed him out of the door and he closed the door behind him.

"And don't come back!" Coach Smith emphatically said to Swish.

Coach Smith turned back to the players and he asked them, "Now, where was I? Oh, yeah." He said to himself.

He looked up at the group and he noticed that Freeze was walking away.

"Where are you going, son?" Coach Smith asked Freeze.

Freeze said nothing to the coach. He just went to sit in the middle of the court in the circle of the court.

Coach Smith asked Freeze again.

"What are you doing, son?" Coach Smith asked Freeze.

"Practice is over, Coach," Freeze answered him.

"What do you mean the practice is over? You been smoking them funny cigarettes or something? We got at least two more hours of practice." Coach Smith informed Freeze.

"Not me, Coach. Not until you call Swish in here and apologize to him." Freeze insisted that the coach do.

"What are you talking about, boy? Apologize to him, you want me to apologize to that freak? When hell freezes over." Coach told Freeze.

Freeze responded to the coach by sitting there in silence.

"Fine, then. You want to give up your basketball career for that retarded bastard. That's fine with me. We will play without you." The coach told Freeze.

Coach Smith turned to the rest of the group and he said to them, "Everyone else, give me five laps around the court."

The team responded to the coach by just standing there idly.

"You heard me. Five laps around the court!" The coach yelled out again at the team.

At this time, JJ went to the center of the court and he had a seat with Freeze. One by one, the rest of the team followed suit.

Coach said to them, "You guys willing to give up the season for him?"

No one said a word. They all sat in silence. The coach stood silently with his arms folded.

Finally, Coach Smith said to Freeze, "OK, bring the little retard-," Coach Smith paused and he rephrased his conversation

He then said to Freeze, "I mean get the young man in here."

Freeze stepped out of the gym and he brought Swish back into the gym with his arm around Swish's shoulders. Swish was still sobbing.

"Calm down, Swish. Coach has something to tell you." Freeze told Swish.

Freeze stood Swish in front of the coach. Coach Smith just stood there without saying a word.

"What?" Coach Smith finally said to them, as if he was at a loss for words.

The rest of the team came to stand with Freeze and Swish.

"Tell him, Coach, that you apologize for being mean to him," Freeze told Coach Smith.

The coach took a hard swallow, looked at Swish, and said to him, "I apologize, son, for being mean to you."

Freeze then said to the coach, "And tell him, Coach, that from now on you will not call him any more names."

The coach said to Swish, "And from now on son, I will not call you any more names."

JJ then added him to say, "And from now on Swish is a part of the team and he will get a uniform."

"Oh, no, that's not going to happen." Coach Smith insisted upon this.

The rest of the team went and sat back down in the circle. Coach Smith stood there defiantly, with his arms folded for a moment.

Finally, Coach Smith said to Swish, "Ok, you are a member of the team and we will get you a uniform."

The team stood up and they cheered. They all gather around Freeze and Swish to celebrate.

"Five laps!" Freeze yelled to the team, while he and the team led Swish to do his first five laps as an official member of the team.

All the players were yelling, "Swish!" "Swish!" "Swish!"

"This is a mutiny." Coach Smith mumbled to the team under his breath.

The season always ended with their team and St. Francis' team going undefeated till the last game of the season. They always ended up playing St. Francis in the regional championship finals game.

For the past three years, St. Francis had defeated them in the regional finals and they went on to win the state championship.

Three years in a row, AT High has lost to St. Francis in the regional finals. JJ, Freeze, and the other senior players felt this was the year they would beat Saint Francis.

The basketball season went as usual. In the three previous years, Amanda Thompkins High (AT High) blew through the competition every year to get to the regional finals. Only to lose to St. Francis by a couple of points in the regional finals game.

Last year they lost in a buzzer-beater by one point. So, this was what they had been waiting for.

Once again here the two teams were. St. Francis and AT High in the regional finals. The referee gave the signal, and the game began. AT High got off to a good start.

After 3 quarters, it looked like AT High might finally win against St. Francis. They were up by 12 points through three quarters, but then disaster struck.

Freeze, their best player, was hobbling on the court. He came to the sidelines. It appeared he had sprained his ankle.

"No more basketball for you today." The team trainer told him.

"Damn!" Freeze said emphatically, as he hobbled to the bench.

"Now what do we do?" Big Mo asked his teammates.

Freeze took the grimace of pain off of his face and he tried to encourage the team by showing a brave face.

"We go kick some ass!" Freeze told the team.

"Who are we!" Freeze yelled to his teammates.

The team yelled out, "AT High," in a less than enthusiastic tone.

"What was that?" Freeze asked them.

"We can do better than that. Now once again, who are we!" Freeze yelled out again.

"AT High!" The team yelled out more enthusiastically this time.

"I didn't hear you! Who are we?" Freeze yelled out to them again.

The team shouted, "AT High!," even louder.

Freeze yelled out, "We ride together!"

JJ yelled out, "We die together!"

The whole team yelled out, "I am my brother's keeper!"

They broke ranks cheering and running out onto the court.

As the game restarted, AT High was putting up a valiant battle, but without their best player, Freeze, in the lineup, Saint Francis started cutting into AT High's lead. The only thing Freeze could do was be a cheerleader on the sidelines.

With AT High's best player sidelined. Saint Francis' players were double and triple-teaming AT High's next-best player. Who was JJ.

With twelve seconds to go in the game, the St. Francis guard hit a three-pointer to put St. Francis up by two points. AT High's coach called for a timeout.

He started setting up a play for JJ. Freeze then remembered how Swish had been shooting the ball from half-court.

"Hey, Coach," Freeze yelled over to the coach, getting his attention.

"Yeah, son." Coach Smith answered him.

"Let's use our secret weapon. Seeing you know with me out of the game they are gonna double team JJ. Let's make a play with our secret weapon." Freeze told the coach.

"And who is our secret weapon?" Coach Smith inquired about Freeze.

Freeze whispered into the coach's ear.

"Oh, no, are you serious?" Coach Smith asked Freeze.

"Trust me on this one, Coach," Freeze told Coach Smith.

The coach looked at Freeze for a second. He then nodded approval of Freeze's plan.

"This had better work." Coach Smith told Freeze.

Freeze told the coach, "Coach, I got this."

Freeze called Swish over and he explained to Swish and the rest of the team the play.

After Freeze explained the play, he told the team to "Break on three."

Freeze yelled to them, "Three," and the team yelled out, "I am my brother's keeper," as they took their positions on the court.

JJ reminded Swish of the play.

"Remember Swish, stand right here in the far corner and when we pass you the ball, shoot towards the basket. Understand?" JJ asked Swish.

"Ok," Swish replied to him.

The horn sounded to restart the game and Swish was led to the far-right corner of the half-court. The St. Francis side of the auditorium began laughing and clowning around.

"Awe looks like a monkey on the court!" Someone yelled out from the St. Francis side.

"You guys going out like suckas'. Putting Special Ed on the court!" Another Saint Francis fan shouted out.

"It's a diversion! Keep your eyes on that JJ, kid!" The coach of St. Francis instructed his team to do this.

Big Mo' took the ball out. He threw the ball to one of the Robinson twins, who quickly threw the ball to Guerrero, who quickly threw the ball to JJ.

When JJ got the ball, three Saint Francis players converged on him. JJ quickly whipped the ball over to Swish, who was standing in the right corner of the half-court line.

With five seconds left in the game, Swish stood there a second holding the ball.

"Shoot the ball!" JJ yelled for Swish to do.

The whole AT bench shouted for Swish to, "Shoot the ball!"

The crowd yelled for Swish to, "Shoot the ball," as the clock wound down, 3, 2,1…

Swish shot the ball. Everything seemed to be moving in slow motion as the arc of the ball descended down toward the basket.

"Swish," was the sound of the ball going through the bottom of the net as the horn to end the game sounded off simultaneously.

First, there was utter silence at the amazement that a person of Swish's stature had made the basket from half-court.

Simultaneously, the AT High crowd and the AT High bench gave out a big roar as they stormed the court. While the Saint Francis team and their fans stood there in shock.

The AT High fans were yelling, "Swish!" "Swish!" "Swish!"

Coach Smith, who was still in disbelief at what had just happened, was standing there next to the coach of the other team. He was still in shock that they had won the game.

The coach of the other team threw his clipboard to the floor and he said, "Beaten by retardo."

Coach Smith approached Saint Francis's coach and he said to him, while he pointed his finger into the coach's face, "His name, is Swish!"

Coach Smith then ran off the court yelling out, "Swish!" "Swish!" "Swish!"

Two weeks later, AT High won the state championship.

Seemed like the month of March came around fast. Like basketball and football, JJ and Freeze were on the baseball team. Unlike football and basketball, they were benchwarmers on the baseball team.

This suited them fine. They weren't really great baseball fans. They were on the team only because it gave them a reason to be out of class. Still, they brought Swish along and he became the team mascot.

Swish really didn't show any special baseball skills as he had shown in the other two sports, other than he was a great water boy and equipment manager.

However, many thought he was a good luck charm. The baseball team went undefeated while Swish was their mascot.

They ended up the season 30 and zero and they won the Triple Crown: The state baseball championship, the state basketball championship, and the state football championship. The first time ever done at AT High in its 80-year history.

The school year kept rolling along. Now the month of May had crept upon them.

CHAPTER 11 THE TALENT SHOW

Freeze and JJ were chilling on a bench in the school Quad. Freeze threw some water out of his water bottle onto JJ's face and Freeze then ran off through the campus. The water smacked JJ in the face. JJ stood up blinking his eyes. He was trying to clear his eyes of the water that had hit him in the face.

"Oh, it's on now," JJ said to Freeze, as he reached into his backpack, and got a bottle of water out of it and he started to chase after Freeze.

The two ran throughout the campus exchanging water tosses against each other. Both of them were laughing and running around carefree. They were not paying much attention to the surrounding area.

JJ aimed a water shot at Freeze. Freeze ducked and the water hit Principal Johnson in the face.

Both of them stopped what they were doing and they stood there in shock in front of Mr. Johnson. JJ took a napkin out of his bag and handed it to Mr. Johnson.

"Well, thank you, sir. Quite refreshing, but, I assure you, I did shower this morning." Mr. Johnson told JJ in jest.

"Sorry, Mr. Johnson, sir." JJ timidly said to Mr. Johnson.

Mr. Johnson told JJ, "Son, come to my office."

JJ gave a look of dismay to Mr. Johnson. Freeze intervened trying to help JJ.

"Really, sir, I started this. This is my fault." Freeze said, as he stepped in and assured Mr. Johnson the misdeed was his fault.

"Very well, I appreciate your honesty. You come to my office, too." Mr. Johnson told Freeze.

JJ looked at Freeze. Freeze just threw his hands up in the air.

The two young men dismally walked behind Mr. Johnson to his office. Both of them were contemplating what the consequences of their misbehaving were going to be.

They arrived at Mr. Johnson's office. Mr. Johnson opened the door for them. The two stepped into his office.

"Have a seat, young men." Mr. Johnson said to them, as he ushered them into his office.

The two young men had a seat in front of Mr. Johnson's desk where two chairs were set before the desk. Mr. Johnson pulled out some papers and he looked over them.

He then looked up at the two young men and said to them, "Young men, despite your immature appearance. I believe you are both brighter than you appear to be right now."

JJ and Freeze were a little confused about where this conversation was going.

"So, young men, I have brought you in here because there is an important task that needs to be done. Do you think the two of you are up to doing a very important task?" Mr. Johnson asked them, as he looked at JJ.

"Yes sir, Mr. Johnson. Anything for you." JJ

told Mr. Johnson.

Mr. Johnson looked at Freeze. Freeze nodded his head up and down.

"Good, young men. Miss Taylor needs some judges for the talent show. Usually, we pick two young men and two young ladies. So, after school today, report to Miss Taylor and she will give you your assignments." Mr. Johnson told them.

"Yes, sir, Mr. Johnson," JJ said to him.

"Yes, sir," Freeze said to Mr. Johnson.

Mr. Johnson went back to reading the paper he had in his hand. JJ and Freeze looked at each other. They were confused as to whether they could leave the office or not.

JJ kept signaling to Freeze to ask him. Freeze kept signaling to JJ to ask him.

Finally, JJ got up enough courage to speak to Mr. Johnson.

He said, "Excuse me, Mr. Johnson, sir."

"Yes, young man." Mr. Johnson responded to JJ.

"Are we free to leave?" JJ inquired of him.

"Young men, the both of you, carry on." Mr. Johnson told them.

Both of them got up slowly in shock that they were not in more trouble. They slowly began to exit the office. Mr. Johnson caught them before they left out of the office door.

"Oh, one other thing, young men." Mr. Johnson said to them.

"Yes sir, Mr. Johnson." They both answered him in unison.

"Please, don't let me catch the two of you clowning around again." Mr. Johnson told them.

"Yes sir, Mr. Johnson." They both said in unison.

They both walked out of the office. They were appreciative of the break Mr. Johnson had given them.

As they exited the office, JJ grabbed his heart and told Freeze, "Man, that was close. The last thing I need to do is get into some more trouble."

"I feel ya' on that. I thought we were done for. I just thank God it wasn't Mr. Jackson." Freeze told JJ.

"Oh, shutter the thought," JJ said to Freeze

JJ then said to Freeze, "Thanks, my homie."

"Thanks for what?" Freeze asked JJ.

"Thanks for not leaving me hanging," JJ told Freeze.

"It was nothing. I learned my lesson from the last time." Freeze told JJ.

The bell rang for their next class.

"Hey, how about White Castle's on me after school?" JJ asked Freeze.

"Sure, after school. I'll see ya, then." Freeze told JJ.

The two embraced and they set off on their separate ways to their classes.

The day of the talent show arrived. It was May 7th. The excitement of the anticipation of Summer break was in the air. Especially for the seniors, who would be graduating that year.

The talent show was an annual event sponsored by Miss Taylor to raise money for school field trips. This was the day the jugglers, the singers, and the want-to-be rappers came out to display their talents.

Not only did JJ and Freeze have to be judges for the talent show, but they were also responsible for selling tickets to the event.

Only seniors could participate in the talent show and the winning prize was two tickets to the senior prom.

Miss Taylor called JJ and Freeze to her room on the day of the talent show. She thanked both of them for their effort in selling the talent show tickets.

She told them that they had sold more tickets than anybody in the time she had been selling talent show tickets.

"Well, you know. We hustlers." Freeze bragged to Miss Taylor.

"And what do you mean by that?" Miss Taylor asked him in a stern voice, with her hands on her hips.

"He speaking for himself, Miss Taylor," JJ told her.

"Way to throw me under the bus," Freeze whispered to JJ.

Freeze then turned his attention to Miss. Taylor.

"Aw, Miss Taylor, I meant that in a good way," Freeze said to her, as he gave Miss Taylor a hug.

She patted him on the back and she told him, "Get on out of here, boy. Trying to finesse me. I am not one of those little girls you be chasing after."

"Naw', ma'am, Miss Taylor. You way finer than them." Freeze told her.

Miss Taylor laughed at him and she told him, "Boy, if you don't get out of here with those dead pickup lines."

Freeze said to her, "OK, Miss Taylor. I'm leaving."

The two of them left her room. After the boys left her room, Miss Taylor took her mirror out and she began looking at her face in the mirror.

As JJ and Freeze were leaving her classroom and walking down the hall. Freeze said to JJ, "She knows she wants me."

"Who wants you?" JJ asked Freeze.

"Miss Taylor, she knows she's hot for me," Freeze said to JJ.

JJ looked at Freeze and he shook his head.

"You are a pervert." He told Freeze.

Freeze told JJ, "Yep, and I'm gonna be a pervert until I'm a dead vert".

Freeze started laughing as he was putting his right hand up to get a high five from JJ. JJ just walked away from him, shaking his head.

"Aw, JJ, you gonna leave me hanging, bruh'?" Freeze asked JJ, as he ran off trying to catch up with him.

The night of the talent show had arrived. The auditorium was packed with faculty members, parents, and students. There were 12 contestants on the stage. Miss Taylor went to the microphone and introduced all of the contestants, along with JJ and Freeze and two other students who served as judges.

The first contestant was dressed like a clown, George Peacock. George came out with his juggling act. He did well all the way to the end. At the end of his act, he dropped one of the balls he was juggling. He got booed off the stage. George took a bow anyway.

The next act was Jeremy Stills, Roger Barnes, and Tyler Martin. They were a rap group that went by the name of XYZ.

In the middle of their rapping, the crowd wasn't too pleased with them. The crowd booed them off of the stage, also.

The next act was Alice Colbert. She did a scene from the play, "Gone with the Wind." She got a lukewarm applause.

The next few acts rolled by quickly until they got to the next to the last act. This act was by Tonya James.

Tonya sang a rendition of Aretha Franklin's, "Respect." She got a rousing ovation after she finished her act.

Finally, there was the last act. This was Maria Consuelo. Maria was a great singer. She was expected to win the competition. After all, she had already appeared at the opera house, singing the aria from the opera, "Carmen," "The Toreador Song."

This time she would sing the aria from the opera, "Evita, Don't Cry for Me Argentina".

She started off the song low-key, but then she began to crescendo as the song continued to the end and she ended the song on a high note. A note so high that you wondered if the glass window panes in the building were going to break.

She got a rousing round of applause. After the last act, Miss Taylor came back to the microphone.

"We will now tabulate the vote." Miss Taylor said to the crowd.

As they were tabulating the votes, there was a buzz in the auditorium of people talking to each other while they anticipated the outcome of the vote.

Suddenly, everybody got quiet, as Miss Taylor came back to the microphone and she said to the audience, "For the first time in this competition. We have a tie between Tonya James and Maria Consuelo. When we have a tie, the audience gets to choose the winner." Miss Taylor informed the audience.

The crowd in the auditorium began to get restless. Some people were shouting "Maria" and others were shouting "Tonya."

The audience appeared to be getting overheated. Miss Taylor and the other faculty members were struggling to keep order in the auditorium. Just as it appeared things were going to get out of hand, music started coming from the piano.

Everyone looked up on stage and they saw Swish playing the piano. He began to sing as he was playing the piano.

He sang, "What the World Needs Now Is Love" by "Hal David."

Swish was singing the lyrics to the song and he was playing the music on the piano. Everybody started to watch him.

Swish turned towards the audience and he said to them, "Come on, everybody, sing."

Everybody began singing the song with Swish. As he finished the first stanza of the song, Swish encouraged the audience to sing one more time.

"Come on, one more time," Swish said to the audience.

Now Swish encouraged the audience to wave their hands in the air while they were singing.

"Wave your hands, everybody," Swish told the crowd.

The whole audience was singing the song now and they were waving their hands in the air. After the second stanza of the song, Swish ended the song.

He got up off of the piano stool, went to the center of the stage, and took a bow. He then went to sit down.

The crowd gave him a rousing applause and a standing ovation.

As things began to quiet down, Maria and Tonya walked back to the microphone together. Maria addressed the audience.

"We, Tonya, and I agree," Maria said as she looked over at Tonya. Tonya nodded her head.

Maria went on to say, "We think that Benjamin should win the competition."

First, the audience got quiet.

Freeze then got up and started yelling, "Swish!" "Swish!" "Swish!"

One by one, the entire audience started yelling, "Swish!" "Swish!" "Swish!"

This took place for about five minutes. Miss Taylor then went to the microphone. The auditorium got quiet again. Miss Taylor addressed the audience.

She said to them, "The people have spoken. The winner of the 1996 Amanda Ellen Thompkins Senior High School talent show is, Mr. Benjamin Swisher." She informed the audience

The audience again broke out into applause and cheers. Swish was congratulated as he walked up on the stage. People patted him on the head as he went to accept his award.

Now Swish was on stage standing next to Miss Taylor.

"Anything you want to say to the audience, Mr. Swisher?" Miss Taylor asked him.

Swish looked around the room at the audience and he said to them, "Thank you, everybody. I love you."

The audience yelled back at him and they said to him, "We love you too, Swish!"

After he accepted his award, Swish made his way over to Freeze and JJ, who were still sitting in the judges' chairs. They both looked at Swish and gave him a hug.

Freeze stepped back from Swish and he asked him, "Where did you learn to sing like that."

Before Swish could answer him, Freeze said to him, "I know. Watching TV, right?"

Swish just nodded his head up and down.

Freeze told Swish, "I gotta' find out what channels you be watching."

CHAPTER 12 SWISH (BENJI) GETS A DATE FOR THE PROM

Now, it was the last week in May. JJ and Freeze were getting ready for the senior prom. They were both at a tuxedo store shopping for a tuxedo.

"Man, these tuxedos are expensive," JJ said to Freeze.

"Yeah, I know. Especially the blue one that I want." Freeze said to JJ.

"I figured you would wear blue," JJ told Freeze.

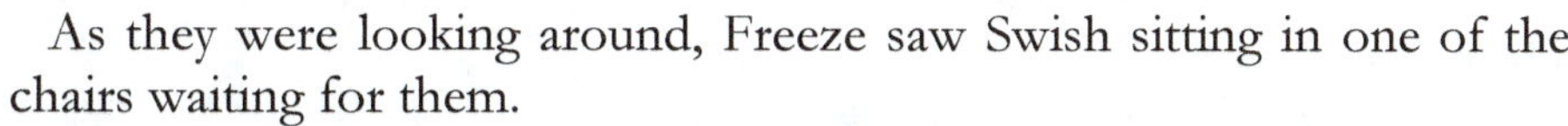

As they were looking around, Freeze saw Swish sitting in one of the chairs waiting for them.

He asked JJ, "Hey, what about Swish?"

JJ answered him and asked him, "What about Swish?"

Freeze said to JJ, "Well, what about a tux for him? He does have two tickets to the prom." Freeze reminded JJ.

"Yeah, that's true, but let's face it. Who is going to go to the prom with Swish?" JJ asked Freeze.

Freeze told JJ, "Just leave that to me."

JJ asked Freeze, "You really think you can get him a date to the prom?"

Freeze told JJ, "If I can't do it, my name is "Attila the Hun". You know those girls can't resist my irresistible charm. They will do anything for me."

JJ said to Freeze, "OK, I'm down wit' it. Let's go for it."

Freeze told JJ, "First thing first. Let's get the little man fitted up for a tuxedo. We have to figure out how we're gonna get some money to pay for it."

"No, we don't," JJ told Freeze.

Freeze asked JJ, "Oh, you got money to get him a tuxedo?"

JJ answered him and he said to him, "Yeah, I do. I still got his $1100 from when we won the basketball game in the lower bottoms."

Freeze asked JJ, "You mean you didn't spend that money?"

JJ told Freeze, "No, I didn't spend that money. That's Swish's money. Would you have spent it?" JJ asked Freeze.

Freeze looked at JJ and he told him, "I take the fifth."

JJ stared at Freeze, with his arms crossed and he gave him a stern look.

Freeze then said to JJ, "Well, I would've thought about it."

Now JJ was standing there in the same position, but now he was patting his foot.

Freeze told him, "Ok, ok, I wouldn't have spent it. Are you satisfied?" He asked JJ.

JJ said nothing. He just nodded his head to Freeze.

Freeze complained to JJ and he said to him, "Man, outta' all the best friends in the world I could get. I get the son of the Pope."

JJ ignored Freeze's comment. He turned his attention back to Swish.

"Anyway, let's get this show on the road," JJ told Freeze.

"Right, Operation Swish. In full effect." Freeze told JJ.

The two of them searched for a tuxedo for Swish. They have him put on a white one with a purple sash.

"Nice, you're gonna be the life of the party," Freeze told Swish.

"Now let's do something about that hair," JJ told Swish.

Freeze and JJ go into the hair store. They find a can of fake hair.

"Let's see, does this match his color?" Freeze asked JJ showing him a can of red hair.

They looked through the cans of fake hair and they found a can of red hair that came close to matching Swish's hair color.

"Perfect," Freeze said, as they sprayed a sample of the fake hair onto Swish's head.

Freeze used the can on Swish's head. He then tried to put the can back on the shelf and he tried to get out of the store without paying for the can of hair.

He looked around to see if anyone was watching. He then quickly put the can back on the shelf.

JJ saw him put the can back on the shelf and told him, "Really, Freeze."

JJ took the can back off of the shelf and he showed Freeze the price on it.

He told Freeze, "$2.99, Freeze. For that, you want to risk taking a trip downtown."

Freeze just threw his hands up in the air, as JJ took the can to the counter and paid for it.

Next, they took Swish to get a haircut. After Swish got a haircut, they took him to buy him some white dress shoes.

"Hey man, you can't be looking more fly than me, now." Freeze joked with Swish, as Swish tried on his white shoes while he was wearing his white tuxedo.

Freeze looked at JJ and he said to him, "OK, now here's the plan. I'm gonna find him a date. You teach him playa' etiquette. Deal?" Freeze asked JJ.

"Deal," JJ said to Freeze, as he agreed with Freeze's plan.

The whole week JJ was mentoring Swish on what to say to a young lady, while Freeze was trying to get someone to go to the prom with Swish.

It was the day before the prom. Freeze met up with JJ and Swish at the playground.

"You find someone, Attila?" JJ asked Freeze.

"Nobody, not even my mother," Freeze said to JJ in a joking manner.

"What happened to your irresistible charm?" JJ asked Freeze.

"Nothing, I just gotta' put it into a little overdrive," Freeze told JJ.

"Yeah, I feel ya'. I've been asking around, too. No luck here, either. Even offered to pay someone. Not happening. I've been rejected in three different languages." JJ told Freeze.

Freeze looked over at the other basketball court. Kayla Smart was shooting the ball around.

Kayla was the center for the girls' basketball team. She stood 6'2" and weighed about 180 pounds.

She had a tall wiry body and she wore manly clothes. It was hard to tell that she was a female.

Freeze looked at JJ and he asked him, "Did you ask her?"

JJ asked Freeze, "Did I ask who?"

"Her," Freeze said to him, pointing over to Kayla.

JJ looked over at Kayla and he said to Freeze, "You talking about her, Kayla? King Kong Kayla. I don't know if you knew this or not, but, Kayla is not into boys. She likes girls."

Freeze told JJ, "I know that, but we are desperate."

JJ ushered Freeze towards Kayla with his hand and he told Freeze, "Be my guest. If you feel bold enough."

Freeze walked over to Kayla, who was shooting the basketball. He called her name.

"Kayla," Freeze said to her.

Kayla stopped dribbling the ball at the sound of her name being called. She answered Freeze.

"What do you want, Freeze?" Kayla asked him.

Freeze said to her, "You're pretty good at basketball, huh?"

Kayla said to him, "Get you a squad and my squad will beat any squad you pick."

Freeze said to her, "Whoa, and confident, too. I love that in a woman."

Kayla said to him, "My girls and I will beat any team you put on the court."

JJ whispered into Freeze's ear, "She ain't lying."

"How about one on one?" Freeze asked Kayla.

"You don't have anyone, male or female, at this school that can beat me in basketball. Not even you, because unlike the boys, who won only one state championship. The girls have won four state championships in a row." Kayla boasted to Freeze.

"She right about that," JJ whispered into Freeze's ear.

"I feel ya' on that," Freeze told her.

"Tell you what. Seeing that you are physically superior to everybody. Let's make this a finesse game. Jump shots only. My friend here, Swish, needs a date for the prom. I hear you are available. So, here's the deal. A game of HOP. You and Swish. You win, name your price. We win, you go to the prom as Swish's date." Freeze told Kayla

Kayla looked at Swish and she then rolled her eyes and she told Freeze, "Even if I dated boys. I damn well sho' wouldn't date small potatoes like him. I've had cats bigger than him."

Freeze said to her, "Name yo' price, Kayla. Tell you what. I'll even throw in a fit for you for the prom and I will pay for it." Freeze told her.

JJ looked at Freeze and asked him, "We will?"

"Yeah, remember, Swish has money saved up. What a better way to spend it on him." Freeze whispered to JJ.

JJ told Freeze, "OK, let's go for it."

Freeze turned his attention back to Kayla and he asked her, "What's the holdup, Kayla? You aren't scared he's gonna' ta' beat ya', are ya'?"

Kayla responded to Freeze by saying to him, "Nobody at this school, can beat me. I'm just scared I'm gonna break his l'il' heart." She told Freeze, while she was laughing.

"Name your price," Freeze told Kayla.

Kayla told him, "OK if he wins, I will take him to the prom. What I get if I win?" Kayla asked Freeze.

Freeze told her, "You get $500."

JJ made a throat-clearing sound and he told Freeze, "Um, um."

He tugged on Freeze's shirt and whispered into his ear, "That's a bit much, isn't it?"

"Come on now, JJ. Have some balls. I got this." Freeze assured JJ.

"Yeah, last time you told me that, we almost got killed." JJ reminded Freeze.

Freeze told JJ again, "I got this."

"It's a deal," Kayla told Freeze.

"OK, a game of HOP. Jump shots only. If Swish wins, you take him to the prom. If you win. We will give you $500." Freeze told Kayla.

Swish and Kayla met on the basketball court on the playground. A crowd gathered around as Kayla and Swish squared off to play a game of HOP. Freeze was holding the basketball.

He handed the basketball to Kayla and said to her, "Ladies first."

Kayla grabbed Freeze by the collar and said to him, "Don't be playing with me, Freeze. If I win. I want my $500."

Freeze answered her standing there with his hands up in the air.

He said to her, "OK, OK, relax Queen Zilla. You're gonna get your money if you win."

Kayla slowly released Freeze's collar.

Kayla took the first shot. She shot from the free-throw line and she made it. The crowd cheered.

Next, Swish shot from the free-throw line. He made it, also. The crowd cheered.

Kayla shot from the right corner. She made it. The crowd cheered.

Swish shot from the right corner. He made it, also. The crowd cheered.

Kayla shot from the left corner. She made it. The crowd cheered.

Swish shot from the left corner. He made it, also. The crowd cheered.

Kayla shot from the top of the key. She made it. The crowd cheered.

Swish shot from the top of the key. He made it, also. The crowd cheered.

The two of them go back and forth making their shots. Each of them was not missing any of their shots.

Finally, Kayla went to the far-right corner. She took a shot. The ball hit the front of the rim and fell to the court. A groan came from the crowd.

Now, for the first time, Swish was in control of where the ball was shot from.

"Now it is Swish's turn," Freeze told Kayla.

Freeze told Swish, "Go to the top of the key."

Swish went to the top of the key. Swish shot the ball. It went straight into the hoop. The crowd cheered.

Kayla shot from the top of the key. The ball went into the hoop and the crowd cheered.

For another 15 minutes, the two exchanged shots, and both of them made their shots.

Freeze pulled Swish to the side and told him, "Swish, this girl is good. You've got to be creative."

"Ok," Swish responded to him.

This time Swish went to the top of the free-throw line of the other court.

"Ooh." The crowd said as they watched him prepare to shoot.

"Wait a minute. Nobody in basketball shoots from there." Kayla complained to Freeze.

"This is not basketball. This is HOP." Freeze reminded her.

"Whatever, I doubt if the funny man can make it from there anyway," Kayla told Freeze.

Swish went and he stepped on the free throw line of the other court. He squared up to shoot the ball. He heaved the ball toward the opposite basket. Everyone's eyes followed the trajectory of the arc of the ball.

"Swish." Was the sound of the ball as it went through the bottom of the net. The crowd erupted into cheers.

Now it was Kayla's turn to shoot. She took the ball to the free throw line of the opposite court. She squared up to shoot the ball. She heaved the ball towards the hoop. The ball was in the air.

"Bong." Was the sound of the ball as it hit the front of the rim and fell to the floor. A groan went through the crowd.

"I believe that's, "H," Freeze told Kayla.

Now it was Swish's turn again. Swish went and stepped on the top of the key of the other court. He squared up to shoot the ball. He heaved the ball toward the opposite hoop. Everyone's eyes followed the trajectory of the arc of the ball.

"Swish." Was the sound the ball made, as it went through the bottom of the net. The crowd erupted into cheers.

Now it was Kayla's turn to shoot. She took the ball to the top of the key line of the opposite court. She squared up to shoot the ball. Kayla heaved the ball towards the hoop. The ball was in the air.

"Bong." Was the sound the ball made as it hit the front of the rim and fell to the floor of the court. A groan went through the crowd.

"I believe that's HO," Freeze told Kayla.

"Whatever," Kayla said to Freeze.

Next, Swish went to the out-of-bounds line of the opposite court. The full length of the court.

"Ooh." The crowd said as Swish prepared to shoot the ball.

Swish squared up and he shot the ball. The crowd was quiet as they watched the ball go straight into the hoop. Everyone began to cheer.

Now, it was Kayla's turn to shoot the ball. Kayla went and set up at the full length of the court. She squared up and she shot the ball the full distance of the court.

"Whoosh," was the sound of the ball, as she shot an air ball.

"That's HOP," Freeze said to Kayla, as he was taunting her by putting his hand in her face while he was hopping around her.

Kayla looked frustrated. She swiped at Freeze's hand, but he was too quick for her, and each time she swiped at him. She missed him.

"Well, well, Cinderfella' is going to the ball," JJ told them.

Freeze added, "With the bride of Frankenstein."

Freeze and JJ gave each other a high five.

Swish walked up to Kayla, got down on one knee, and asked her, "Would you go to the prom with me?"

He reached out to Kayla with his right hand.

The crowd went "A-a-w."

A frustrated Kayla knocked away Swish's hand and she just stormed off of the court. Freeze went to stand by Swish.

"That's ok, Swish, baby boi'. You gotta' date for tomorrow night." Freeze assured him.

Freeze turned around and reminded Kayla of the time they were picking her up.

"Kayla, be ready at five," Freeze told her.

Kayla threw her hands up in the air and she kept walking away. She gave Freeze the middle finger, as she walked away.

"Aw, baby. Let's not get personal, now." Freeze told her.

Freeze turned his attention back towards Swish.

"Come on Swish. We gotta get you ready for the prom tomorrow." Freeze told him.

JJ and Freeze escorted Swish off of the playground to JJ's house.

CHAPTER 13 THE PROM

The last day of May had arrived. May 31, and today was the day of the senior prom. It was at some ritzy hotel downtown.

Most seniors didn't go to school that day. They were at home preparing for that night. Next to graduation, the senior prom was the biggest day of their lives, so far.

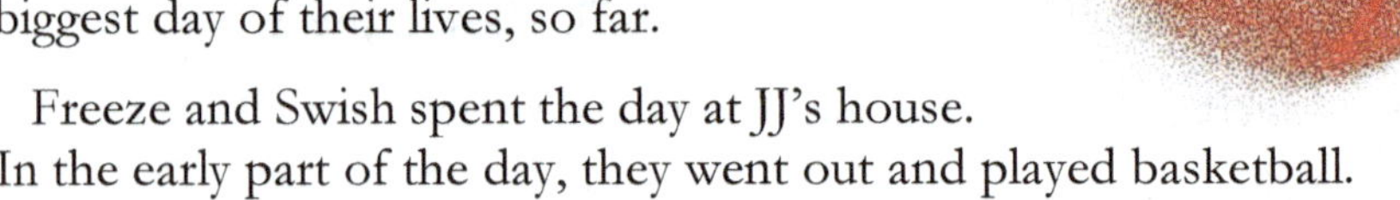

Freeze and Swish spent the day at JJ's house. In the early part of the day, they went out and played basketball.

At about noon, they went to the burger shop. Freeze and JJ spent some time going over with Swish how to treat a lady.

"Hey, it's 1 o'clock. We need to get to the house." JJ told them.

"OK, give me a couple of minutes to finish my shake and I'll be ready," Freeze told JJ.

The guys finished up at the burger shop, and they went to the bus stop. On the way to JJ's house, they stopped downtown to pick up their tuxedos.

After the boys picked up their tuxedos, they headed back to JJ's house. The time was 3 o'clock when they got back to JJ's home.

Freeze decided to take a nap on the couch while JJ went over some etiquette lessons with Swish.

JJ was so entrenched in his lessons with Swish that he didn't keep track of time.

Fortunately, he had set the alarm clock. The alarm clock went off at 5:00 pm. JJ ran to the couch and he woke up Freeze.

"Get up, Freeze. Time to get dressed." JJ told Freeze.

Freeze got up and he went to take a shower.

JJ went back to Swish and he helped him get dressed. Swish got undressed down to his underwear. JJ helped him first put on his pants.

He then helped him put on his shirt. After JJ finished helping Swish get dressed, he went to make sure that Freeze was up. He heard Freeze in the shower.

JJ returned downstairs to check on Swish. He looked at Swish standing there. Swish had gotten a black spot on his white pants in the little time JJ had left him alone.

"Aw, man!" JJ yelled out.

"Swish what did you do to your pants!" JJ asked him.

"I don't know," Swish said in his childlike voice.

Freeze came out of the bathroom draped in a towel.

"OK, what did Swish do? I heard you all the way upstairs." He told JJ.

"He got a dark spot on his pants," JJ complained to Freeze.

"Oh, is that all? I thought he had set the house on fire or something." Freeze said as he was laughing at the situation.

"Let me get dressed and I can handle that." Freeze assured JJ.

"OK, but hurry up. The limo will be here any minute." JJ told Freeze.

Freeze got dressed. He then came downstairs and looked at the small dark spot on Swish's left pant leg.

Freeze told JJ, "Never fear. Freeze is here."

"OK, Iceman. What we gonna do about this situation?" JJ asked Freeze.

Freeze took a look at the spot-on Swish's pants.

He then said to JJ, "Do you know for a young man? You sure fret a lot. Now watch this."

Freeze pulled a small bottle out of his pocket.

"Presto," Freeze said, as he showed JJ a small vial.

"And what, pray tell. Might I ask, is that?" JJ asked him.

"This, my homie. Is white-out. Never leave home without it." Freeze informed JJ.

Freeze opened the white-out and he started applying it to the black dot on Swish's pants until the dark spot couldn't be seen.

"There, good as new." He told JJ.

"And you just happen to have a bottle of white-out in your pocket?" JJ asked Freeze.

"Sure, never know when it's needed. Comes in handy. You might make a mistake on paper. You might need to change something that you wrote down." Freeze told JJ.

JJ interrupted him and he said to him, "You might need to cheat on a test or do graffiti in the school bathrooms."

"C'mon now, bruh'. That's confidential." Freeze told JJ.

The three young men finished getting dressed.

Freeze stood Swish up in front of the mirror and he said to him, "Look at you, smooth. All dressed up. You clean as a cool summer breeze, boi'."

Swish stood there in the mirror smiling.

Freeze added, "Don't worry about who's gonna be King of the Prom. You know that's gonna be me." Freeze told Swish, sporting his blue tuxedo with his blue cool daddy hat on.

"You do understand that I am going to be King of the ball?" Freeze asked Swish.

Swish nodded his head and he answered, "Uh huh."

Freeze told Swish, "See, my main man. With answers like that. You're gonna be my friend for a long time."

A big grin came on Swish's face. Freeze got JJ's attention.

Freeze looked over at JJ and he said to him, "Hey, JJ. Look at my man here, Swish. Ain't he the coolest cat you've ever seen?"

JJ was in another mirror fixing his tie. He glanced over quickly at Swish and Freeze.

"Yeah, Freeze. He is sharp as a tack." JJ responded to him.

JJ then went back to fixing his tie.

As the young men were doing last-minute touch-ups to ready themselves for the prom. They heard a car horn blow outside.

"Limo's here!" Freeze yelled out to JJ.

The three young men gathered their belongings and they headed out to the limousine. They were going to meet their dates at Freeze's girlfriend's house, Rebecca Charles.

JJ's date was Joyce Powell, and of course, Kayla Smart was Swish's date.

They arrived at Rebecca's house at about 5:45 pm. JJ and Freeze ran up the stairs and they rang the doorbell. Rebecca's mother opened the door and she greeted them.

"You young men have a seat right here on the couch and the girls will be down shortly." She told them.

When she walked away, Freeze told JJ, "I told you they wouldn't be on time."

"Yeah, it's like an unwritten rule for women, huh?" JJ said to Freeze.

"More like it's in their DNA," Freeze told JJ.

Freeze gave JJ a high five. The first one down the steps was Joyce. As she sauntered down the steps, the young men couldn't take their eyes off her. How stunningly beautiful she was in her lavender dress.

"Hello, gentlemen." She said politely to them.

The young men stood there gawking at her. Admiring her beauty.

Next down the stairs was Rebecca. She floated down the stairs in her pink dress. Once again, the boys gawked at the sight of her beauty.

"Welcome to my home." She said to them, as she greeted them.

"Kayla will be down shortly." She informed them.

Five minutes go by. Still, the boys haven't said a word to the ladies. They just sat there with their eyes wide open.

Next, Kayla came down the stairs. Kayla was wearing a white chiffon dress. She was a little unsteady on her feet, in that she was not used to wearing high heels.

The boys were really stunned at her beauty. Until this time, they considered Kayla as one of the boys. She was tall and slender and she was very attractive. She stumbled awkwardly down the stairs because she had to get used to wearing high heels

"Never thought Kayla would look so good." Freeze thought in his mind.

As soon as he saw Kayla, Swish jumped up and met her at the bottom of the steps.

"It is my pleasure, sweet princess. To be taking you to the prom." Swish told her.

He got down on one knee and he asked her, "Would you allow me to put this corsage around your ankle?"

"Whatever," Kayla said to him abruptly.

She was unmoved by what Swish was asking her permission to do. Swish put the corsage around Kayla's right ankle.

After Swish placed the corsage around Kayla's ankle, Rebecca and Joyce looked at Freeze and JJ expectantly.

After she stood there a couple of minutes, Rebecca addressed the young men.

"Well," Rebecca said to Freeze.

"Well, what?" Freeze answered her.

Rebecca crossed her arms and she asked him, "Do I get a corsage?"

"Oh, yeah," Freeze said to her.

He pulled his corsage out of his backpack and he attempted to hand it to her. She took a deep breath and she looked down at her ankle.

"Oh, yeah," Freeze said to her.

He got down on one knee and he put the corsage on Rebecca's right ankle.

Now it was Joyce's turn. She looked at JJ. JJ looked puzzled at first. Joyce then looked down at her ankle.

"Oh, yeah," JJ said to her.

He pulled out his corsage and he put it on Joyce's ankle.

"Gurl', who would have thought that the slow guy was gonna be the most romantic one tonight," Rebecca told Joyce.

"I'm telling you, gurl'," Joyce said to Rebecca, as they high-fived each other.

"OK, ladies. Our chariot awaits." Freeze told them.

The limousine was a white, stretch, vehicle. Freeze and JJ ran out to the limousine, leaving everyone else behind.

Swish walked up to Kayla and he held out his hand and asked her, "May I escort you, my princess to the limousine?"

Kayla told him, "Oh, Negro, please. I can walk by myself. Thank you anyway." She said to him, with an attitude in her voice, as she pushed his hand away from her.

The four of them who had been left behind, made their way to the limousine. JJ and Freeze were already inside the limo when the other four got to the limo.

Swish walked ahead of the group of ladies. He opened the limo door for Kayla. Kayla just nodded her head to him, as she got into the limo.

Rebecca and Joyce stood outside of the limousine. Rebecca made a throat-clearing sound as if to give the guys a hint to come open the door for them.

JJ finally got the hint. He jumped out of the car and he opened the door for Joyce.

He was followed by Freeze, who got out of the car and opened the door for Rebecca.

Rebecca asked them, "Are you sure that you guys taught Swish the ropes, or did Swish teach you guys the ropes?"

"C'mon', Rebecca, baby. I'm just excited to see you. I just slipped up a little bit." Freeze told her.

JJ also chimed in.

"Yeah, Joyce. You girls are stunningly beautiful today. We have never seen you girls dressed up like this."

"OK, you guys get a pass today, but I hope the rest of the night goes better than this," Rebecca told them.

"Relax, drinks are on me. Look here we got Dr. Pepper, Pepsi, 7-Up, and Coke." Freeze told them, as he opened up the cold box in the limo.

Freeze popped open a soda and he started drinking it as the limo pulled off on the way to their destination.

The limousine pulled up to the hotel. Once again, Swish got out of the limo and he opened the door for Kayla.

Freeze and JJ followed suit. They got out of the limo and they opened the door for the ladies they were escorting.

Swish put his hand out to help Kayla out of the car. Kayla pushed his hand out of the way.

Rebecca and Joyce were being assisted out of the car by Freeze and JJ.

Rebecca told Kayla, "Gurl', you better recognize a good thang' when you see it."

Kayla told her, "If you think he's so good, you take him."

"Naw', gurl'. Unfortunately, I made a commitment to Bozo, here." Rebecca told Kayla.

The six of them entered the Plaza. The music was already blasting. They presented their tickets to the maître d'. He led them to their table. Their table was close to the door.

When they got to their table, Swish pulled a chair out from under the table for Kayla to sit in. She reluctantly took a seat. Swish began to take a seat next to her.

"Please, don't sit next to me." She told Swish.

"Yes, my princess," Swish said to her.

Swish went and stood up next to the dance floor next to some support beams

"Man, Kayla. You kinda' being harsh on my man." Freeze told Kayla.

Kayla said to him, in a defiant voice, "I agreed to come to the prom with him. That's it."

"Lighten up, Kayla. Come on, the little guy is sensitive. You might hurt his feelings." JJ informed her.

Kayla, with her arms folded, just sat in her chair ignoring them.

"Whatever," Kayla responded sharply to them.

In the meantime. There seemed to be some excitement over on the dance floor.

"Let's go check it out," Freeze told them.

"Come on, Kayla. Let's go check it out." Rebecca encouraged her to do.

Kayla just threw her right hand up, rejecting them.

They (JJ, Freeze, Rebecca, and Joyce) went to check out the dance floor. They have to wade through a crowd of people to make it to the dance floor.

When they got to the dance floor. They went into shock. Swish was on the dance floor, doing every dance from the "Chubby Checker, Twist," to the "Michael Jackson, "Moonwalk."

Everybody was yelling, "Go Swish!" "Go Swish!" "Go Swish!" "Go Swish!"

Somebody yelled out, "Electric slide, electric slide!"

Swish led the whole group in doing the electric slide.

"Are you seeing this?" Freeze asked JJ.

JJ said to Freeze, "Pinch me. I gotta be dreaming."

"Ow!" JJ said as Freeze pinched him.

"I didn't really mean for you to pinch me. That's just an ol' expression." JJ told Freeze, as he rubbed his arm.

Freeze looked at JJ and he smiled at him and he hunched his shoulders as if to say, "Sorry."

After they were done with the electric slide, all of the girls wanted to dance with Swish.

After four hours on the dance floor, the band took a break. Everyone went back to take a seat at their tables.

When they got to their table. Rebecca looked around and asked them, "Where is Swish?"

"I don't know," Joyce answered her.

Freeze said to them, "Maybe he went to the bathroom."

JJ said to them, "I'll go check."

Just when JJ started to get up and go check the restroom, a voice came from the stage. It was Swish. JJ sat down after he heard Swish's voice on the microphone. Swish addressed the audience.

He said, "This is for the young lady that I was so graced to come to the prom with. I am not even worthy of drinking out of her slippers."

Swish then turned his attention towards Kayla.

He said to her, "Kayla, my princess. This is for you."

He then walked down off of the stage playing the guitar and he went into a rendition of the Righteous Brothers, "Unchained Melody".

He began to sing in a sensuous smooth voice.

He sang to her, "Oh, my love, my darling…"

All of the girls began to scream and they ran towards the stage. Some of them took off their corsages and they threw them at Swish.

Kayla was just looking starry-eyed, as Swish was singing to her.

Swish slowly descended from the stage, as he played the guitar. He was serenading Kayla, as he was walking from the stage towards her.

Kayla was sitting down, mesmerized by Swish, as Swish moved closer and closer to her.

The crowd departed like Moses departed the Red Sea to make a path to let Swish through to Kayla. On his way to Kayla, Swish pulled out one of the roses from one of the flower displays in the room. He slowly walked towards Kayla. All eyes were on Swish and Kayla, as Swish made his way to her.

As he came to Kayla's feet. He went down on one knee and he handed her the rose he had picked from one of the flower displays. By now tears were streaming out of Kayla's eyes.

She pulled him up to his feet and she let him sit next to her. Swish held her hand. Kayla just sat there looking at Swish starry-eyed.

The band returned to the dance floor. The guitar player retrieved his instrument from Swish. He winked his eye at Swish as he returned to the stage. The band leader got on the microphone.

He said, "OK, ladies and gentlemen. Time for the last song of the night. If you got to get on the dance floor. Now is the time." The bandleader informed them.

About fifteen to twenty girls lined up at Swish's table. They were hoping that he was going to give them the last dance.

To their demise. Kayla stood up and she said to them, "Excuse me, ladies. This is my date."

All of the young ladies quickly backed away from the table. No one wanted any part of the likes of King Kong Kayla.

Kayla got up to walk, but she stumbled a bit since she was not used to wearing high heels.

Swish gently helped her sit back down and he took her shoes off of her feet. He then escorted Kayla to the dance floor.

When they got to the dance floor. Couples were already dancing on the dance floor to, "Ribbon in the Sky," by "Stevie Wonder".

Kayla and Swish squeezed onto the dance floor between the other couples. You couldn't help but notice the short Swish dancing with a tall Kayla.

Despite their height differences. They were so smooth together. Soon everyone on the dance floor ceded to this couple dancing to, "Ribbon in the Sky," by "Stevie Wonder."

Swish and Kayla had an audience surrounding them as they were now the only couple on the dance floor dancing. The music ended with Swish swinging Kayla around and he caught her in his arms.

The students cheered as the music ended and everyone went back to have a seat at their tables.

Now cake and punch were being served. Kayla was sitting next to Swish now. She could not take her eyes off of him.

Someone walked up on stage. It was Jason Torres, the school student body president. He had an announcement to make.

"Okay, ladies and gentlemen. Before we leave here tonight. Here are the results of the King and Queen of the Prom." He told them

Jason read from a piece of paper.

He told the crowd, "The most exciting couple of the 1996 Amanda Ellen Thompkins High School senior prom of 1996 is," there was a drumroll, and Jason Torres then announced the two winners.

"Kayla Smart and Benjamin Swisher." He said to the crowd.

First, everyone got quiet.

Freeze then jumped up on his feet and started yelling, "Swish!" "Swish!" "Swish!"

Everyone then started yelling, "Swish!" "Swish!" "Swish!", as Swish and Kayla made their way up to the podium. They were crowned King and Queen of the Prom by Jason Torres.

Jason said to them, "Come on, say a few words."

First, Kayla got up to speak. Kayla thanked the crowd for the honor. She told everyone how she had never intended to come to the senior prom and how she had the best time of her life.

They then handed the microphone over to Swish. Everyone got quiet. Swish looked around at the crowd.

He then said to them, in his timid voice, "I love everybody, and I just want everybody to be my friend."

Initially, the crowd was silent.

Freeze then said to him, "We love you too, Swish!"

Everybody then started saying to Swish, "We love you too, Swish!"

Some of Swish's classmates carried Swish off of the stage back to his seat, as the crowd chanted, "Swish! "Swish!" Swish!"

The festivities wrapped up and the young people started back to the parking lot. They went back to their limos.

The six of them got into their white limo that was waiting for them. This time JJ and Freeze quickly opened the door for their dates.

Swish had already opened the door for Kayla, and they were sitting in the back of the limo.

JJ and Joyce were sitting in the center and Freeze and Rebecca were sitting up front.

They first got to Kayla's house. They dropped Kayla off and everyone said their goodbyes.

"Goodbye, Swish," Kayla said to Swish, as she gave him a kiss on the cheek.

"Goodbye, my princess," Swish said to her, as he jumped out of the limo to open the door for her.

"Goodbye, Kayla." They all said to her.

 Kayla took a couple of steps towards her house. She then returned back to the limo.

"Oh, I forgot something," Kayla said to them.

She opened the back door of the limousine.

"What did you forget, Kayla?" Rebecca asked her.

"I forgot this." She said to them, as she grabbed Swish by the arm and she pulled him out of the car.

She then slammed the car door and she said to them, "Don't wait up for him."

She literally dragged Swish to her house.

"Bye, Swish." The two girls said to him in unison.

Swish waved goodbye to them, as he was being pulled by Kayla to her house.

"Bye, Swish." The girls said to him again in unison.

"Oh, boy. What's he got that I don't have?" JJ asked the girls.

"I don't know, but I wish I could find out," Joyce told him.

"Yeah, gurl', Kayla is lucky tonight," Rebecca told Joyce, as she and Joyce gave each other a high five.

"I'm telling you, women," JJ said as he shook his head.

The next house they got to was Rebecca's house. Rebecca and Joyce both got out at Rebecca's house. Joyce was spending the night with Rebecca.

"Good night ladies." JJ and Freeze said to them.

Now Freeze and JJ were alone with the driver in the limousine. Freeze made a comment about how the night went.

"Man, that was some crazy ass night," Freeze told JJ.

JJ was quiet at first.

JJ then said to Freeze, "Tell me the truth now, Freeze."

"Tell you the truth about what?" Freeze inquired of JJ.

"The truth about how you feel about Swish. You are a little jealous of him. Aren't you? I mean he stole your thunder tonight." JJ told Freeze.

Freeze stopped and thought about what JJ was saying to him.

He then asked JJ, "Why would I be jealous of Swish?"

JJ said to him, "C'mon', Freeze. All this year you've been talking about being the prom King and you know you are always the life of every party. Swish took that away from you tonight."

Freeze looked at JJ and he said to him, "You know, normally you would be right, but actually, I'm cool wit' it. Not being prom King was worth seeing Swish being happy."

"Are you fo' real?" JJ asked Freeze.

"Yeah, I'm fo' real," Freeze told JJ.

"Wow, you have changed," JJ told Freeze.

"That's a good thing, right?" Freeze asked JJ.

JJ nodded his head to Freeze. The limousine drove up to JJ's house. JJ and Freeze got out and went into the house.

The next morning, it was about 12 noon, when JJ got up. He went downstairs. Freeze was still sleeping on the couch. JJ shook Freeze, but he was unable to arouse him.

JJ went to look in the cupboard for some cereal. He heard a car horn blow from outside. JJ went to the door, still dressed in his boxer shorts and T-shirt. He opened up the front door and there was Swish getting out of the car with Kayla.

"Bye, Swish," Kayla said to Swish, as she blew him a goodbye kiss.

Swish turned around and he blew her a kiss back. Swish then walked up to JJ's house. He had a big grin on his face.

"Well, Swish, how was your night?" JJ asked him.

Swish did not say a word. He just walked by JJ with a big grin on his face.

He walked in and just had a seat on the loveseat that was across from Freeze, who was still sleeping.

"Well, Swish. What did you do last night?" JJ asked Swish

Swish just sat there smiling.

"You went over to Kayla's?" JJ asked Swish.

Swish said nothing. He just nodded his head.

"You get in bed with her?" JJ asked Swish.

Swish didn't say a word. He just nodded his head still He was still smiling.

"You went to sleep with her?" JJ asked Swish.

Swish just nodded his head. He was still smiling.

JJ stopped and thought.

He then said to Swish, "Ooh, Swish. You mean you..."

Before JJ could ask the question. Swish started nodding his head vigorously. He had a big grin on his face.

JJ told him, "Swish, you are a naughty boy."

Swish nodded his head even more vigorously.

"Wait till I tell Freeze," JJ told him.

Upon hearing his name. Freeze woke up yawning.

"Wait till you tell Freeze what?" Freeze asked JJ between yawns.

"Wait till I tell you who's not a virgin anymore before we are," JJ told Freeze.

"Who, my boi', Swish?" Freeze asked JJ.

"I know that Swish got down with Kayla," Freeze told JJ.

"How did you know?" JJ asked Freeze.

"C'mon now, JJ. I know you're not that naive, are you? The girl came and practically dragged him out of the car like a caveman drags his woman. What else you think she was coming back to get him for? To serve him milk and cookies? Freeze asked JJ.

Freeze turned his attention towards Swish and he said to him, "Look at you, Baby Boi'! Come on over here my man and give yo' potna' some dap."

Swish walked over to Freeze and gave Freeze a fist pound.

Freeze looked at JJ and said to him, "And speak for yourself, homeboi'. My flytrap was sprung a long time ago."

JJ looked over at Freeze and said to him, "Really, I guess I'm the only Gumby around here, then."

Freeze put his arm around Swish and he said to him, "Welcome to manhood, Mr. Swisher. We gonna have ta' get our friend over there laid. So, he won't be so uptight."

"Okay," Swish responded to him.

"Now that you are a man, like me. What can I get you?" Freeze asked Swish.

"Some ice cream," Swish told Freeze.

"You are the man. Ice cream, it is, on me. Rock n Roll (Rocky Road), right?" Freeze asked Swish.

 Swish vigorously nodded his head.

 C'mon, Mr. Swisher." Freeze said as he put his arm around Swish's shoulder.

Freeze looked over at JJ and he asked Swish, as he pointed to JJ, "You don't mind if this child comes along with us?"

"Whatever," JJ responded to him.

With JJ on one side of him with his right arm wrapped around Swish's left shoulder and Freeze on the other side of him with his left arm wrapped around Swish's right shoulder, Swish was escorted to the ice cream shop.

 On the way to get ice cream, Freeze asked Swish, "Where did you learn to get down with a woman?"

 Freeze paused, and before Swish could answer the question, he asked him, "Don't tell me, TV?"

Swish shook his head from side to side to indicate, "No."

Freeze said to him, "Oh, I was getting ready to say. I'm gonna start spending more time at your house watching TV with you."

After they left the ice cream shop. The two of them (JJ and Freeze) walked Swish home.

On their way back to JJ's house, after they had dropped Swish off at his house, JJ asked Freeze, "Can you believe that Swish got down with Kayla."

Freeze told JJ, "Yeah, that is an unbelievable thought that Kayla got down with any boy. Yet alone Swish."

A few minutes later, JJ asked Freeze, "Do you think you could get down with a girl who liked girls?"

Freeze answered JJ laughing and he said to him, "Her sister and her potna'. All at the same time."

JJ told Freeze, "You know what? I should've known better than to ask you that question. You are a pervert." JJ told Freeze.

"Yeah, I'm gonna be a pervert, till I'm a deadvert," Freeze said to JJ while he was still laughing.

JJ stood there shaking his head, as he watched Freeze laugh.

As his laughter ebbed, Freeze looked at JJ and he said to him, "Race you to your place?"

"Alright," JJ told Freeze.

They get into a starting position.

"Ready on three," Freeze told JJ.

JJ and Freeze got into the starting position. Freeze began to count.

"Ready, One, three," Freeze said quickly, as he took off running He left JJ behind.

JJ just stood there shaking his head. He then ran off after Freeze.

CHAPTER 14 SOMETHING IS WRONG

It was now a week after the prom. Six days to go till graduation. JJ was outside watering the lawn. Freeze came by to visit him.

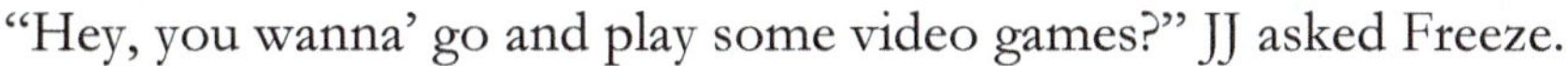

"Hey, stranger. Haven't seen you since two hours ago in class." Freeze jokingly said to JJ.

"What's up, my homie?" JJ asked Freeze.

The two gave each other a fist pound and a manly hug.

"Hey, you wanna' go and play some video games?" JJ asked Freeze.

"Sure, why not? I don't have anything, but time to kill." Freeze said to JJ.

"C'mon in here so I can school you, young fella'," JJ told Freeze.

"Not in this lifetime," Freeze told JJ.

The two of them got the video games out. They set it up and they began playing.

As they were playing, Freeze asked JJ, "How is our little playboy doing? I miss the little fella'."

JJ responded to him by asking him, "Who, Swish? I don't know. I miss him, too. I haven't seen him in two or three days. Last time I spoke to his mother. She said he needed to get some rest and that she was going to keep him in a few days."

They continued to play their video games. They had been playing video games for about an hour when the phone rang. JJ stopped the game to answer it.

"What are you stopping the game for? I was winning." Freeze complained to JJ.

"Phone ringing. It might be Moms." JJ said to Freeze.

JJ ran to answer the phone.

125

"Okay, but don't let that be the reason you lose this game," Freeze told JJ.

JJ spoke to someone on the phone. He then hung up the phone and returned to play video games with Freeze. He had a puzzled look on his face.

"Who dat' was?" Freeze asked JJ.

"That was Swish's Mama," JJ answered Freeze.

"What's up with Swish? He okay?" Freeze asked JJ.

"I don't know. His mama said he was in the hospital. She said he had a relapse. What does that mean?" JJ asked Freeze.

"I don't know," Freeze answered JJ.

Freeze then asked JJ, "What hospital is he at?"

"County General," JJ answered him.

"Let's go see about my little homie," Freeze told JJ.

The two left JJ's house and they caught the bus to the east side of town to the hospital. They both sat on the bus joking around, trying not to show how worried they were about Swish.

"County General." The bus driver yelled out, as they arrived at their destination.

"Here's our stop," JJ told Freeze, as he nudged Freeze, who had almost gone to sleep.

They both exited the bus and they started walking towards the hospital.

"Man, what could be wrong with my little sidekick?" JJ asked Freeze.

"Don't fret. He's a trooper. He's gonna be alright. That's a strong little dude." Freeze assured JJ.

They reached the front of the hospital entrance and they approached the front desk. A hefty Black lady dressed in all white, with a nurse's cap on, sat at the front desk. Freeze approached her.

The lady looked up at Freeze and with an attitude in her voice she asked him, "May, I help you?"

Freeze told her, "I come to see Swish--."

He caught himself in mid-sentence and he said to the lady, "I mean Benjamin Swisher."

She looked up the name on her clipboard. She then looked over her black-rimmed glasses, eyed the two of them standing there, and asked them, "And who might you be?"

"We are friends of his," JJ told the lady.

The lady looked down at her clipboard again, then looked back up at them and said to them, "Sorry, family only."

"But, ma'am. You don't understand. His mother—, JJ tried to explain the situation to her, but she interrupted him.

"Family only." She said to him again, as she cut his conversation short.

"Lady, don't you have a heart?" Freeze asked her.

"Young man, don't you have any ears? Family only." The lady repeated herself to them while pointing her fat stubby index finger towards the exit.

Both JJ and Freeze turned around and they exited the hospital. JJ began to descend the stairs outside of the hospital. Freeze grabbed JJ's left shoulder and he stopped him from leaving.

"She can't do that to us," Freeze complained to JJ.

"Looks like she can to me," JJ responded to Freeze.

"Come on now. I know you not going out like that." Freeze told JJ.

"Yeah, what do you suggest?" JJ asked Freeze.

Freeze whispered into JJ's ear. Both of them reentered back into the hospital. Freeze nudged JJ. He then walked up to the front desk. The lady at the desk looked up from the magazine she was reading and she confronted them again.

"Oh, you again. Family only, I said." The lady told them.

"I know ma'am, but I gots' ta' pee," Freeze told the lady, as he jumped around like he had ants in his pants.

"Well, I suggest you better go home, young man." The lady advised him to do.

"C'mon, lady. Home is a 30-minute bus ride away." He told her.

"Too bad. Now outta' here." She told him.

"Okay, lady. Guess I am gonna have ta' take a whiz right here on the floor." He insisted as he unzipped his pants.

"Young man." The woman said to him as she gasped and she held her bosom.

"Okay, lady. What's it gonna be? The bathroom or a new floor job?" Freeze asked her.

"Okay, to the bathroom with you. Then off be with you." She told Freeze, as she buzzed the door open and the two of them began to enter the facility.

"Uh-uh, you, only." She told Freeze, motioning for him to come in and holding her other hand up halting JJ from entering.

JJ looked at Freeze and he just shook his head.

"Plan B," Freeze whispered to JJ.

Freeze entered the hospital and started down the hallway toward the bathroom. The lady watched Freeze until he entered the bathroom.

She then turned her attention towards JJ, who stood by the door. The lady kept a suspicious watch on JJ.

"I got my eye on the two of you. Y'all up to no good." She told JJ.

The two stood there for about three minutes watching each other. JJ struck up a conversation with the lady.

"One thing for sure, lady," JJ said to the lady.

She looked up at him, with a look of attitude on her face.

"You can't watch the both of us at the same time," JJ told her.

Just as he said those words, Freeze came dashing out of the bathroom and he reached over the counter and pressed the door release button. A loud buzzer sounded off and JJ darted through the door.

"Security, security!" The lady yelled out, as she threw objects and hit them with all types of thrown things.

"Relax, lady," Freeze told her, as he dodged everything from books to papers, to pens and pencils.

As JJ came through the door, both of them ran down the hallway to the elevator. They waited for what seemed like hours for the elevator, as the lady at the front desk called for security.

"Ding." The elevator came just as security got to the front desk. The boys saw the lady pointing in their direction. Security hurriedly came towards them.

"Hurry, into the elevator," Freeze told JJ, as he shoved JJ into the elevator.

He quickly pushed the button to close the elevator doors and he pushed a floor, just as a security personnel reached the elevator. The elevator ascended to the fourth floor.

"Now what?" JJ asked Freeze.

"Relax, buddy. Don't you have any confidence in me?" Freeze asked JJ.

"Okay, what's the plan?" JJ asked Freeze.

"We need to find out what room Swish is in," Freeze told JJ.

"Really, now that's a novel idea. You think of that all by yourself?" JJ asked Freeze sarcastically.

The elevator door opened on the fourth floor.

"Come on," Freeze whispered to JJ, as he pulled JJ out of the elevator.

The two of them were looking into the rooms down the hallway each way. A noise came from the end of the hallway. It was security looking for them. Freeze grabbed JJ by the arm and he pulled him into a janitor's closet. Security passed them up.

JJ asked Freeze, "Why is it every time I'm with you, seems like I'm running for my life?"

Freeze told JJ, "That's because you have a boring life, and I put some spice into it."

JJ requested Freeze, "Yeah, well put a little more sugar and a little less pepper, please."

"Okay, the coast is clear. Let's make our move." Freeze told JJ, as he peeped out of the closet door.

The two eased their way out of the closet into the hospital hallway. Just as they felt they had gotten away from security, a towering tall security person showed up from around the corner of the hallway.

They turned to run in the other direction. Only to run into another security guard.

"Yeah, you two troublemakers." The tall security guard said to them, as the two security officers cornered them.

The other guard said to them, "All right come on with us."

JJ tried to plead their case.

"You don't understand. Our friend is here. He might be very sick. We just want to see him." JJ tried to explain to the guards.

"Yeah, yeah sure." The tall security guard said to them.

"Don't bother to try to reason with these marks. They were born with no hearts." Freeze told JJ.

Just at that time, someone called their names.

"Foster, Jenkins." A lady's voice was heard calling their names.

The two young men looked up to see Swish's mother standing in the doorway of one of the rooms.

"Is there a problem, Officer?" Miss Swisher asked the two security guards.

"You know these two?" The tall security guard asked Miss Swisher.

"Yes, I know these two. They are good friends with my son. I had my son's doctor's permission to let them come see him." She told the two officers.

The tall security guard looked at the other guard. The other guard nodded his head.

He told Miss Swisher, "Yes, ma'am. If you can vouch for them. They can visit."

The officer handed the two young men over to her.

"Thank you, sir." Miss Swisher told the officers.

The security officers were now leaving. Freeze jumped at the officers like he was going to do something physical to them.

"Would you stop? Don't mess it up. We in." JJ reminded Freeze.

"Yeah, he didn't know who he was messin' wit'," Freeze told JJ, as he looked at JJ and he took his thumb across his nose.

JJ told Freeze, "You know what? I'm gonna get you some professional help when we get out of here."

"Oh, an NFL contract?" Freeze asked JJ.

JJ looked at Freeze and he just shook his head.

"Well, you said professional help. How much more professional than the NFL can you get?" Freeze asked JJ.

"Come this way, young men." Miss Swisher told them.

The young men walked into a room. Lying in the bed was Swish. He had all types of tubes and gadgets making beeping noises coming out of him and hooked up to him.

"Is he okay?" Freeze asked Miss Swisher.

Miss Swisher told him, "I'm afraid not, Mr. Foster. You see, Benji has leukemia. He's been dealing with it for five years now. I don't want to lie to you boys. He is not gonna be with us for long."

Both JJ and Freeze looked at each other in shock. Freeze then grabbed Miss Swisher's hand and he just held it.

"Can he say anything?" JJ asked Miss Swisher.

"You can try. He has been in and out of it." She informed them.

JJ walked up to the bed next to Swish and he quietly spoke to him.

"Hey, buddy. Can you hear me?" JJ asked Swish, as he kept trying to arouse him.

After five minutes of talking to him, Swish slowly opened his eyes. A big grin came on his face when he saw JJ.

"Hi," Swish said to JJ.

He then asked JJ, "Are you my friend?"

JJ grabbed Swish's hand and he said to him, "Yes, Swish. I am your friend, and Freeze is also here. He's your friend, too."

Freeze came over and he grabbed Swish's other hand. A big grin came on Swish's face, as he spoke to Freeze.

"Are you my friend?" Swish asked Freeze.

"Yes, Swish. I am your friend, too." Freeze told Swish.

"Friends for life," Freeze added.

JJ put his hand out to give Swish a fist pound. A feeble Swish put his hand out to fist-pound JJ's hand.

Freeze put his hand out to get a fist pound from Swish and Swish gave him a fist pound, also.

"I'm here for you, buddy," Freeze told Swish.

A big grin came on Swish's face. He then went back to sleep.

"Okay, boys. Let my boy get some rest." Miss Swisher told them.

The two boys turned and they gave Miss Swisher an embrace.

"I want to tell you, young men. I appreciate what you have done for my boy." She told JJ and Freeze.

"You made these the happiest days of his life." She added.

"No, Miss Swisher. However much we did for your boy. It will never match what he did for us. He made these the happiest days of our lives." Freeze told her.

JJ nodded his head in agreement with what Freeze had said. The two of them said their goodbyes to Miss Swisher and they headed off to the elevator.

When they got to the main lobby. They ran into the lady at the front desk again. The lady began to scold them.

"Next time." The lady began to say to them in a sharp stinging voice.

They looked up at her with their sad faces. She stopped saying what she was getting ready to say.

Sensing their sadness, she said to them, "God bless you two."

They just walked by her without saying a word.

As they left out of the exit. Freeze looked at JJ and he said to him in a low-key voice, "Hey, JJ."

"Yeah, Freeze," JJ answered him in an even sadder voice.

"Would you think less of me if I cried right now?" Freeze asked JJ.

JJ told Freeze, "I was about to ask you the same thing."

The two of them sat on the bench outside of the hospital and they both wept. The next day, Swish passed away.

CHAPTER 15 RETURN TO THE LOWER BOTTOMS

The morning after Swish died was Saturday morning. Freeze came over to JJ's house. JJ was still in bed. Freeze tried to get his friend out of bed.

"Get up, hood rat," Freeze said to JJ, as he shook him trying to get him up.

"Leave me alone," JJ told him, as he turned over in the bed and he put the covers over his head.

Freeze snatched the cover off of JJ.

 "Come on, JJ. Get up." Freeze told him.

"Man, you are annoying. Why don't you just disappear?" JJ told Freeze.

"Nope, you ain't gonna get rid of me that easy," Freeze told JJ.

Freeze continued to shake JJ.

"Come on we got something to do," Freeze told JJ.

JJ sat up in the bed rubbing the sleep out of his eyes.

"What now? And how did you get into the house?" JJ asked Freeze.

"Oh, Mom was leaving just as I came. She let me in." Freeze told JJ.

"I'm gonna have ta' have a long talk with Mom," JJ told Freeze.

"Aw, quit. You so crazy. C'mon', I got a plan." Freeze told JJ.

"Oh, God. Here we go. Another one of your crazy schemes. What are we doing this time, Freeze?" JJ asked him.

"Get up and get dressed, and I'll tell you on the way," Freeze told JJ.

JJ got up and got dressed. He came outside and met Freeze, who was waiting outside with a basketball. They started walking down the street.

"Okay, what are we gonna do?" JJ asked Freeze.

"We are gonna go to the lower bottoms to earn some money," Freeze told JJ.

"I'm outta' here," JJ told Freeze, as he turned around and he started back home.

"Come on, JJ." Freeze pleaded with him.

JJ was now backpedaling talking to Freeze.

"Are you serious? We just almost got killed down there. Is money that important to you?" JJ asked Freeze.

"I'm not getting the money for myself. I'm getting the money for Miss Swisher." Freeze told JJ.

JJ stopped backpedaling and he started slowly walking back towards Freeze.

"You are getting the money for Miss Swisher?" JJ inquired about Freeze.

"Yeah, fam. For Miss Swisher." Freeze repeated himself to JJ.

"Wow, what a nice thing to do," JJ said, as he slowly walked back towards Freeze.

JJ had made it back to Freeze.

He asked Freeze, "Okay, two things. What's the plan and who we gonna have as our third person?"

"You worry too much. I got this." Freeze told JJ.

"Yeah, last time you said you got this. You really got this. I ended up running like Jesse Owens in the Olympics and you almost ended up hamburger meat." JJ told Freeze.

At that moment, they heard someone calling their names. They looked up the street and Big Mo, the center from the high school basketball team, was coming up the street.

"Didn't I tell you I got this?" Freeze told JJ.

The two of them greeted Big Mo with an embrace.

"Hey, fellas'. I'm all in. Anything for lil' Swish. My l'il' potna' dude." Big Mo said to them, as he kissed his index finger and he pointed it up to the sky.

"That was a great little guy," JJ added.

JJ turned towards Freeze and he said to him, "I'm in, but this time, I'm not abandoning you."

Freeze said, "We ride together."

JJ said, "We die together."

All three of them said, "I am my brother's keeper."

"I feel ya," Freeze told JJ.

The three of them headed off to the lower bottoms. They went to the basketball courts. All eyes were on them. A lot of the guys remembered them from the last time they were there.

Freeze looked around the vicinity. He saw the two thugs that had jumped him. He pointed them out to JJ and Big Mo.

"Those are the two guys who jumped me," Freeze told them.

"So, what are we gonna do?" JJ asked Freeze.

"Well, for one. We gonna stick together and leave the rest to me." Freeze told JJ.

"Okay, you remember what happened last time we left the rest to you. You ended up in the hospital." JJ reminded Freeze.

"Relax, JJ. I got this." Freeze told JJ.

JJ looked up in the sky as if he were praying.

He then gave Freeze that, 'Okay, I'm depending on you' look."

The basketball games began shortly after they arrived at the park. Just as before, the guy in black collected the money from them.

"Two hunned' a game. The stakes are higher this time around." The man in black informed Freeze.

Freeze handed the man ten $20 bills.

After the man took the money from Freeze, he looked Freeze in the eyes and said to him, "Hard headed, huh youngsta'? Didn't learn from last time."

Freeze said nothing to the man. He just nodded his head.

The man laughed and he told Freeze, "Okay, choir boy. It's yo' funeral."

The games went as last time. JJ and his team have swept through the other teams to qualify for the last game. They have already earned $2000. The final pot had $4000 in it. If they win that they would walk away with half of that pot plus the $2000 they have already won. A total of $4000. Again, there's a break in the action.

During the break, Freeze huddled up with his team and he whispered his plan in their ears. He told them what they were going to do once the game was over.

The final game started. JJ and his team got off to a slow start. They were trailing 16 to 10, but now Freeze and JJ got hot. They began to catch up. After a scoring spree by Freeze and JJ. The score was now 20 to 20.

Now that the two guards, (JJ and Freeze), were hot. The other team could no longer double-team Big Mo, the center, in the middle, as they had been doing.

Freeze and JJ kept feeding Big Mo under the basket. Big Mo scored the last four points of the game and JJ and his team had won the game. They went to collect their money.

The guy with the toothpick in his mouth slowly counted out $4000 in $20s to Freeze. Once he finished counting the money out to them. The man hurriedly left the park in a rush.

The three of them readied themselves to leave the park. As they try to leave, they turn to face about eight guys who have surrounded them.

"You J-cats thought y'all could come o'er yere' on our turf and strip us? You gots' us twisted." The big guy with a patch over his eye said to them, as he flicked out a switchblade.

Several of the other guys surrounding them flicked out switchblades, too.

The three guys, Big Mo, JJ, and Freeze stood together in solidarity. The two groups stood there in a standoff. They stared each other down for a couple of minutes. They (JJ, Freeze, and Big Mo) were relieved to hear a familiar voice call them from afar.

"Hey, Freeze!" A voice came to them from the outskirts of the park.

In the distance, six guys wielding baseball bats were approaching the park. The guys that surrounded them turned to see who was coming. It was Slim and Big Baby and four other guys. All of them were wielding baseball bats.

"Hey, Slim. What brings you to these parts of town?" Freeze asked Slim.

Slim told Freeze, "I was trying to get a baseball team together. There are only six of us. I need you three to make a complete team."

Slim's party walked through the guys that have JJ, Freeze, and Big Mo surrounded. Slim walked up to Freeze and the two of them embraced.

Slim looked at the guys who were surrounding JJ and Freeze and Big Mo and he said to them, while he was waving his bat, "Hey, ladies. Why don't you get your gals together and play my guys in some baseball?"

One by one the group surrounding them started to disperse.

"What, y'all' don't like baseball? Man, that's un-American." Freeze told them.

Freeze and Slim looked at each other again. They embraced each other one more time.

"Man, I didn't ever think I would be glad to see yo' ugly face," Freeze told Slim.

"Oh, yeah. Yo' girlfriend like it." Slim told Freeze, as he was rubbing his hand across his face.

Slim then asked Freeze, "Well, am I still an asshole?"

Freeze told Slim, "Yeah, you are an asshole. Ain't no cure fo' that"

Slim stepped back and looked at Freeze with a funny look on his face.

"But, you're a good asshole," Freeze added.

A big grin came upon Slim's face and he told Freeze, "I will take that. That's progress."

All the young men greeted each other.

Slim then said to Freeze, "Let's get you out of here safely. We're gonna walk all the way through these parts with you till you get to our hood."

Freeze showed Slim how much money they had made.

He then told Slim, "Okay, we got $4000. We can share $2000 with you and your guys, but the other $2000, we gotta' give to Miss Swisher."

Slim told Freeze, as he looked at the money in Freeze's hand, "Normally, my commission is 20%, but this is for li'l man. My boys and I pass. Matter of fact we gonna' add to the pot. Ain't that right, fellas'?" Slim said to the group of guys with him.

Each of the guys with Slim gave Freeze $20. JJ, Freeze, and Big Mo were escorted by Slim and his crew until they made it back to their hood.

When they got back to their neck of the woods, everybody said their goodbyes and they all went their separate ways.

JJ and Freeze took the money they had gotten playing basketball to Miss Swisher. Including the money Slim and his boys had donated to them. They had more than $4000 to give to Miss Swisher.

"I don't know how to thank you. This will pay the cost of his funeral. Now all I have to do is raise money for his plot." She told them.

"What do you want us to do?" Freeze asked her.

"You two have done enough. Thank you, very much. I will have to figure this out myself." Miss Swisher told the two young men.

Freeze and JJ left after they gave Miss Swisher an embrace. On the way back to JJ's place, Freeze mocked what Miss Swisher had said to them about they had done enough.

"You two have done enough. To hell we have. We need to get the job done. Who does she think she is?" Freeze asked JJ.

"I believe she is his mother. The person that gave birth to him." JJ reminded Freeze.

"Doesn't matter. Once I start a job. I finish it. She needs our help, and dammit', she's gonna get it. Whether she wants it or not." Freeze told JJ.

JJ said to Freeze, "Okay, Superman. What do you suggest?" And I don't wanna hear anything about going back to the lower bottoms

"I suggest we take a collection up at school," Freeze told JJ.

OK, let's get started Monday morning." JJ told Freeze.

It was now Monday morning. JJ and Freeze were asking their classmates to give donations for Swish's services.

At about noon, Mr. Johnson called for them to come to his office. The two young men entered Mr. Johnson's office, not knowing what to expect.

"You two young men, have a seat." Mr. Johnson said to them.

The two young men had a seat. Both of them were trying to figure out what they had done wrong.

Mr. Johnson said to them, "I hear you two are conducting an unauthorized fundraiser activity at the school."

JJ looked at Freeze and Freeze looked back at JJ.

Freeze finally told Mr. Johnson, "Mr. Johnson, we're just trying to raise money for Swish's funeral."

Mr. Johnson looked at Freeze and he said to him, "Well, on the record, young men. It is my duty to tell you, gentlemen, that unauthorized fundraising is not allowed on school grounds. Do you guys understand?"

"Yes sir, Mr. Johnson." They both said to him in unison.

"We will stop right away," JJ told him.

Mr. Johnson then said to them, "Now that I've done that. Off the record, you gentlemen are doing a fantastic job, and here's my $20 donation for Swish's fundraiser. If anybody asks you. I don't know anything about it."

JJ and Freeze looked at each other with big grins on their faces.

"Yes sir, Mr. Johnson," They both said to him at the same time.

"Thank you, Mr. Johnson," JJ told him.

"Thank me for what?" Mr. Johnson asked JJ.

"You know, helping with Swish's fundraiser," JJ told Mr. Johnson.

"What fundraiser?" Mr. Johnson asked JJ.

A bewildered JJ stood there staring at Mr. Johnson until Freeze gave him an elbow in the ribs.

Freeze then covered up JJ's mouth and said to Mr. Johnson, "What he meant to say was have a nice day, sir."

Freeze then pulled JJ out of the office with his hand still over JJ's mouth.

"Have a nice day, young men." Mr. Johnson said to them."

"Have a nice day, sir." The muffled voice of JJ said as Freeze escorted him away from Mr. Johnson's office with his hand still covering JJ's mouth.

As they left the office and they stood outside in the hallway.

Freeze told JJ, "Learn when to stop talking."

"My bad." A bashful JJ said to Freeze.

"C'mon, we still got work to do," Freeze told JJ.

JJ and Freeze collected donations for Swish's services all the way until the last period of school. By the end of the day. The two of them have raised another $6000, including donations from Swish's teachers.

At the end of the school day, they took the money to Swish's mother. She was so appreciative of their efforts.

She told them, "Now, boys. I only need $3000 of this. You can take the other $3000 back."

Freeze looked at Miss Swisher and he said to her, "Look, Miss Swisher. With all due respect. We raised this $6000 for you, and if it's alright with you. We gonna leave this extra $3000 with you. What you do wit' it is up to you."

Freeze looked around the house and he said to her, "Looks like you need a new couch or some new drapes. It's up to you, but the extra $3000 is yours, ma'am."

Miss Swisher looked at JJ.

JJ threw his hands up in the air and he told her, "Sorry, ma'am. He's stubborn like that."

Miss Swisher smiled at them and she told them, "You young men are saints. How can I ever repay you?"

Freeze told her, "Now that you mentioned it. You could fix us a batch of those famous fudge brownies you make for PTA nights."

JJ nodded his head in agreement with Freeze, while he rubbed his belly and licked his lips.

"You got it, young men. I will have a batch ready for you tomorrow." She told them.

The two boys gave Miss Swisher a hug. They then left her home.

The next day was Wednesday. The day before senior graduation. Miss Taylor called JJ into her classroom when she saw him in the hallway, as he was leaving to go home.

"I have your grade." She told JJ.

"You do? Is it passing?" He inquired of her.

"Remember, I deducted from your grade during the concert, right?" She told JJ.

"Yeah, I know. I just want to know if it's passing?" JJ asked her.

She showed JJ his grade. It read A+.

"Wow, Miss Taylor. An A+?" He asked her.

"Yes, JJ. An A+." She told him.

"Wow, really? That's awesome." He told her in disbelief.

"What you did for Mr. Swisher was nothing short of a miracle. You deserved an A+." She told him.

JJ gave her a hug and he turned to leave the classroom.

He turned back to her and he told her, "You're wrong, Miss Taylor."

"Why do you say that, JJ?" She asked him.

"Because it's not what I did for Swish. It was what Swish did for me." He told her.

Miss Taylor smiled at JJ and she said to him, "You did a lot of growing up this year, didn't you?"

JJ nodded his head and he turned and left out of the room.

CHAPTER 16 ODE TO SWISH

That brings us to this moment.

Here he was at the podium of his graduation, June 12, 1996. One day before his 18th birthday. He was reflecting upon what had really happened that year. Preparing to give the valedictorian speech for his class.

Not for himself, but for someone else. Lord knows he was not an academic genius.

No, this was for someone more deserving than himself. A special person who had changed the way he looked at life.

He was giving the speech in his stead. Surely an honor. As he stood there waiting to speak, he reflected upon how they had come to this moment. It seemed so long ago.

"Good morning, my fellow students and faculty and administrators and parents and honored guests."

"My name is Jonathan Jenkins. Here I am giving the valedictorian speech. This speech is much more deserving of someone else. His name was Benjamin Swisher."

"I met Benjamin Swisher close to the first day of school. At the time I thought how odd he was. I thought how weird a person he was."

"But now I realize that Benjamin was the epitome of the slogan, "You can't judge a book by its' cover.""

"Benjamin was the most talented, the smartest, the most gifted, but more important, the most loving, most caring, person you could ever want to meet."

"You know we stand here and judge each other on how great we look and how many nice clothes we have and the fancy cars we drive and how much money we have and how much jewelry we have."

"Not, Benjamin. He didn't want or care about any of those material, earthly things. Benjamin just wanted to be your friend."

"Now that I look at it. I look at all of us and I realize we are the weird ones. We are the odd ones. Now that I look at it. Benjamin was the only normal person on earth."

"I believe God put Benjamin on this earth as a role model to us to show us how we're supposed to treat each other. To show us the important things on earth. Love, respect, and kindness. Benjamin was all those things wrapped up into one package."

"Do you know the Bible says, in Hebrews 13:2 KJV, 'Be not forgetful to entertain strangers; for thereby some have entertained angels unawares'."

"Swish was an angel put on earth on loan to us by God to come show us how we should be living. We didn't realize what a gift we had until God took him back."

"I'm going to miss the little fella'. Tagging around with me. My little shadow. Blowing up my game, because the girls thought he was cuter than me."

"Benji, if you can hear me. Yo' best friend is gonna miss ya'." JJ said, as he kissed his two fingers and he pointed them up into the sky.

He then went and touched the seat that was reserved for the valedictorian of the class and he went to his seat and sat down.

As he went to have a seat, Freeze stood up and he started yelling, "Swish!" "Swish!" "Swish!"

And the whole crowd began to chant "Swish!" "Swish!" "Swish!"

A week after graduation, they had Swish's funeral. Eight guys from the school. Four from the basketball team and four from the football team, including JJ and Freeze, were pallbearers.

After the funeral, Freeze and JJ went and sat in the park. The two sat there reminiscing about the school year.

"Man, that was some send-off for Benji. Wasn't it?" JJ said to Freeze.

"Yeah, I know. Swish was something else." Freeze said to JJ.

They sat there in silence for a minute.

JJ then said to Freeze, "Man, did you see Kayla? Dressed up in a widow's garb. Hat with black veil included."

"Yeah, man. I saw her. Did Swish turn her out or what?" Freeze said to JJ.

They gave each other a high five.

JJ then said to Freeze, "It was about 1000 people there at his service. Even the mayor of the city."

"Man, Swish went out like a boss," Freeze told JJ.

"That's for sho'," JJ told Freeze.

"When I go out. That's how I wanna go out." Freeze said to JJ.

A moment of silence went by.

Freeze then said to JJ, "I sure was mean to him."

"What you talking about?" JJ asked Freeze.

Freeze told JJ, "I was. I hung him on the flagpole and I busted water balloons on him."

"There you go. Being down on yourself. Trekking down Misery Road." JJ warned Freeze.

"I was though," Freeze told JJ.

"You know what, Mr. Sad Sack. I'm not gonna let you dog yourself out like that. Because of you, Swish was on the basketball team and football team. Man, how you stood up to Coach Smith that day. Man, I would rather stand up to a pride of hungry lions than stand up to Mr. Smith.

And because of you, Swish went to the senior prom, with a date and he didn't die a virgin." JJ told Freeze.

They gave each other a high five on that.

"And because of you, he had a decent funeral. Man, what are you talking about? You made the last days of his life the best days of his life." JJ told Freeze.

Freeze thought about what JJ had said to him.

"Freeze then told JJ, "Yeah, I did."

Again, there was a moment of silence between the two of them. Freeze broke the silence between the two of them.

He told JJ, "I got to admit something, though. Lil' man made me grow up into a real man."

"You got that right. He did the same for me." JJ told Freeze.

The both of them sat there in silence for a moment again.

JJ then told Freeze, with a sigh, "Yeah, I'm gonna miss him still. I don't think I'm gonna smile again for a long time."

"Oh, really? Well, I'm gonna fix that for you." Freeze told JJ, as he reached into his backpack.

"You are? What magic potion you got you going to fix it with?" JJ asked Freeze.

"Watch this. The magic potion is called H_2O." He said, as he got a bottle of water out of his backpack and he dumped it on top of JJ's head.

Afterward, Freeze grabbed his backpack and took off running. JJ was huffing, trying to catch his breath from the water running over his face.

As he gained his composure, he got a bottle of water out of his own backpack and he said, as he got up to chase Freeze, "Oh, it's on now."

JJ then went running after Freeze.

Epilogue KAYLA'S SURPRISE

Four years later, in March 2000.

Freeze and JJ were at JJ's house playing video games. They were both home for Spring break.

Freeze was going to Michigan to play football and JJ was going to USC playing basketball. At this time, the two were on Spring break and they were at JJ's house on the computer playing video games.

"We're back to school in two days," Freeze told JJ.

"Yeah, me to USC and you to Michigan," JJ told Freeze.

"One more semester to go," Freeze told JJ.

"We then will be graduates," JJ said to Freeze.

"Yeah, we gonna whoop y'all ass when y'all come to play us next week," Freeze told JJ.

"Yeah, just be glad that I'm playing basketball and you are playing football. I would have yo' number." JJ told Freeze.

"Yeah, talk is cheap," Freeze told JJ.

At that time, the phone rang.

"I gotta' answer that. It might be Moms." JJ told Freeze.

"Yeah, don't let that be the reason that you get whooped in this game," Freeze said to JJ.

JJ answered the phone. He came back with a puzzled look on his face and he told Freeze, "That was Kayla on the phone."

"Oh, really. What did she want? I haven't seen her in quite some time." Freeze told JJ.

"I don't know. She said she had something important to show us and she needed us to come over right away." JJ said to Freeze.

"Okay, did she leave her address?" Freeze asked JJ.

"Yeah, it is right here. 2600 Fairmont Drive." JJ told Freeze.

"Okay, we can walk over there. That's just down the street." Freeze told JJ.

The two headed for the address written down on the paper.

"I wonder what she wants?" JJ said as they walked to her house.

"I don't know. But we gonna find out." Freeze told JJ.

Freeze and JJ came up to the address Kayla had given them. Freeze rang the doorbell. Kayla answered the door in what looked like PJs.

"Hey, how my homies doing?" Kayla inquired of them.

They all embraced and the two of them walked into her apartment.

"Forgive my appearance, but I have someone I want you to meet. Hold on." Kayla said to them, as she went to the back of her apartment.

She went back to her bedroom and she brought out a bright-skinned, little freckled-faced, boy, with red hair. He looked to be about three or four years old.

"Oh, Kayla. You are babysitting, huh?" Freeze asked her, as she was holding the little boy's hand.

"Not exactly," Kayla told them.

"What do you mean, not exactly?" JJ asked her.

"Well, fellas'. This here is Benjamin Thomas Swisher Jr." She told them.

They both ogle wide-eyed down at the little boy, who stood before them.

The little boy asked them, "Would you be my friend?"

Freeze just stood there gawking at the little redhead boy, while JJ passed out.

"JJ, you okay?" Kayla asked JJ.

"JJ!" Kayla yelled at JJ again.

Kayla then looked at Freeze and yelled at him, "

Freeze don't just stand there. See about your friend!"

Freeze and Kayla stooped down and tried to revive JJ.